DIRTY PUCKING PLAY

USA TODAY BEST SELLING AUTHOR
CALI MELLE

Copyright © 2024 by Cali Melle
All rights reserved.
No part of this book may be reproduced in any form or by any electronic or mechanical means, including information storage and retrieval systems, without written permission from the author, except for the use of brief quotations in a book review.
This book is a work of fiction and any resemblance to any person, living or dead, or any events or occurrences is purely coincidental. The characters and story lines are created purely by the author's imagination and are used fictitiously.
Cover designed by Cat Imb, TRC Designs
Edited by Rumi Khan
Proofread by Alix Cowell

STAY IN THE KNOW!

Sign up for Cali's newsletter to stay up to date for all things involving her books!
www.calimelle.com

―――――

Did you know that Cali has a Patreon?
If you like exclusive book covers, never before seen content, getting access to books before they're released, NSFW/SFW artwork, among other things, you're not going to want to miss out on this!

PLAYLIST

Breakfast - Dove Cameron
Meddle About - Chase Atlantic
RUNRUNRUN - Dutch Melrose
Fallen Star - The Neighbourhood
Meddle About - Chase Atlantic
WHAT JUST HAPPENED - The Kid LAROI
Delicate - Taylor Swift
Moon & Back - Nic D
Nervous - The Neighbourhood
Stuck On You - Giveon

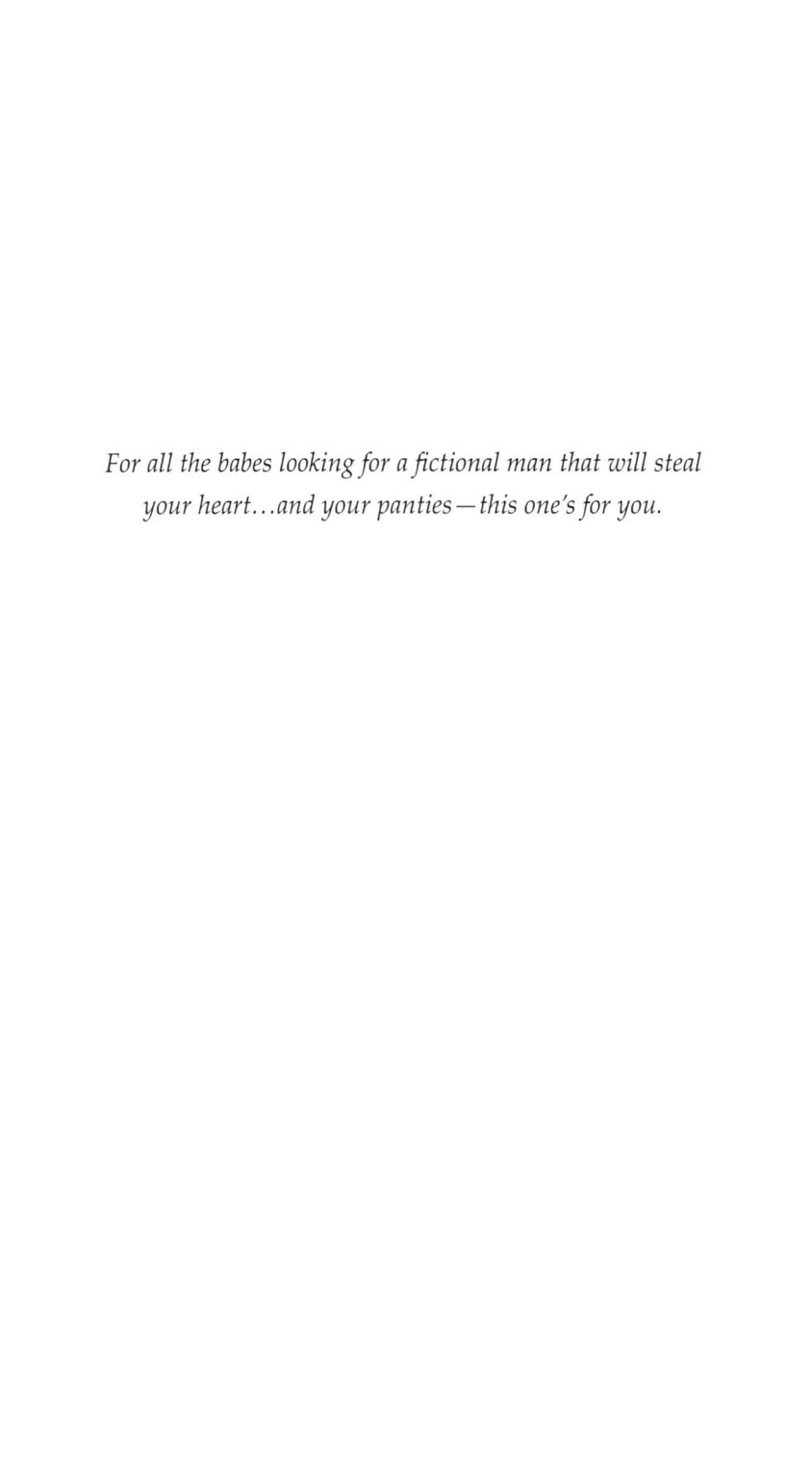

For all the babes looking for a fictional man that will steal your heart…and your panties—this one's for you.

CHAPTER ONE
MAC

"Are you coming to the family skate tonight?" Nico asked me as we walked out into the parking lot after practice. Wes and Lincoln were following behind us, both of them listening in. The air was thick with humidity, wrapping itself around me. Even though we were in the middle of fall, it still felt like how summer felt in the Northern States.

I shrugged as we reached my car and I unlocked it. "None of my family is here, so it seems kind of pointless."

"We're all your family," Wes said with a smile. "You should just come."

Lincoln nodded as he leaned back against the side of my car. "Come on, Sullivan. Don't be all sad and shit. You're not the only one who doesn't have family here. Just come hang out with the rest of us."

I stared at him for a moment before looking at Nico

and Wes, who both seemed to be waiting for an answer. A sigh of defeat escaped me and I shrugged with indifference. "Fine. But only because you guys are being so damn persistent."

Nico smiled and Wes winked. "Good answer."

Lincoln moved away from my car as I pulled open the door and the three of them said their goodbyes before disappearing to their own vehicles. I climbed inside, feeling a touch of disappointment, but I tried to ignore it. I hated the family skating events the team did. They only did them twice a year—as we got closer to the holidays and toward the end of the season.

My immediate family lived in Canada, so I didn't expect them to fly thousands of miles just to come skate for one night. I never actually asked them either. I was used to being so far away from them that it wasn't really a thought anymore. They saw me when I was back in the country for games or if I went home for some time during the off-season. My ex lived in my hometown, so it wasn't exactly my favorite place to visit.

Orchid City was my home now and I was just trying to make the best of being alone here.

My condo was just on the outskirts of the city. Since it was just me, I didn't need anything big, but it was definitely a decent size. The building was huge, with two condos on each floor. As I opened the door, there was a blue-gray body on the other side, wiggling back and forth as his tail was wagging.

"Hey, bud," I greeted Thor, my pit bull who looked like he was smiling up at me as I crouched down to pet him. He was always excited whenever I got home, and he licked at my face, almost knocking me down as laughter spilled from my lips. He was now two years old and still acted like a puppy.

After I moved to Orchid City and bought my condo, I realized how lonely it was living in this vast space by myself. I needed something to fill the emptiness, something to help with the loneliness, and I wasn't in the market for settling down with a woman.

So, one day I ended up at the local shelter and found myself leaving with a malnourished pit bull puppy that someone had found on the side of the road. Thor filled the void; he filled the empty space in my life. It wasn't the same as having another person around, but he offered companionship and that was more than enough for me. I didn't want the complications that came along with dating, so I kept everything superficial with anyone I ever showed interest in.

Relationships were fleeting. They never lasted. Love wasn't a tangible thing. It was more of a mirage than anything.

After giving Thor some attention, I headed through the house with him hot on my heels until I let him out onto the balcony. He wasn't out there for long before he was whining at the door and I let him back in. I didn't have to be back at the arena until after dinner, so I settled on the couch and fell into a dreamless sleep after the exhaustion from practice settled in my bones.

I was the last one to get on the ice, but no one seemed to notice. I glanced around as I slowly began to skate, watching everyone as they were grouped off with their own little families. Nico and Harper were over by the goal line. I watched as his head tipped back and he laughed loudly as Harper's feet almost went out from under her. I couldn't help but smile as I thought about how far they had come.

I may not have believed in love, but they had something special. Something I think everyone was looking for in life. A connection that is deep, that is filled with love… it almost seemed too good to be true.

Then there was Wes and Charlotte. It still blew my mind that he had actually settled down. Lucky for him, he had met his match in her. Charlotte was her own person and Wes was simply caught in her orbit.

Lincoln was single like me, but his twin sisters and one of their boyfriends had come to skate with him. They seemed like the safest bet because I wasn't about to insert myself into a third wheel situation. My feet moved, the muscles in my legs contracting and relaxing as I powered over to where the four of them were.

"There he is," Lincoln said with a grin as he hung back and watched his sisters for a moment. His youngest sister, Eva, was a figure skater, so she was fluidly moving across the ice, ignoring everyone. His other sister, Darya, was trying to help her boyfriend and it was quite comical to watch the two of them. The twins knew how to skate but it was clear that Darya's boyfriend had no idea what he was doing. "Don't mind him." Lincoln laughed as he waved at his sister's boyfriend. "I only brought him along for comic relief."

"Thank God, because I was beginning to feel like the one who was a joke here."

Lincoln rolled his eyes dramatically. "Please. You're not the only person who is single here, so get over it."

"Trust me, I count that as a blessing."

"You and me both," he said with a laugh as he began to skate backward. I followed along with him and we both began to move around the rink. As we finished one lap around the arena, I saw Coach Anderson in the center and he was talking to his wife who was standing unsteady on her skates. It wasn't often that the man smiled, but he looked happy and at ease with her beside him.

As we skated past him, a whirlwind of midnight-colored hair caught my eye. She was skating backward around the center of the rink, moving effortlessly. I was mesmerized, completely captivated, as my feet began to slow. Lincoln noticed I wasn't beside him and shortened his strides before skating up beside me.

"Who's that?" I asked him as I continued to watch her with growing curiosity. Her strides were elongated and there was an elegance to the way she moved as she shifted away from the center of the ice. She wasn't a figure skater, that much was clear.

Lincoln clicked his tongue. "That's Anderson's daughter. From what I heard, she used to play hockey and got injured in college."

My eyes trailed after her and I momentarily lost my edge, but quickly recovered so I didn't end up falling flat on my face. "I didn't know he had a daughter."

"Because he doesn't talk about her much. Supposedly her brother refused to play hockey and Anderson had high hopes for her when she got into the sport instead."

I tore my gaze away from her and looked at Lincoln with an eyebrow raised. "How do you know all of this?"

He shrugged. "I overheard some of the guys talking one day when they saw her here with him. I don't know how they knew about her, I didn't ask questions. Do you really not pay that much attention?"

I didn't, but now I was.

"I'm not nosy like you and Wes."

He stared at me for a moment as our coach's daughter skated past, grabbing my attention once again. I allowed myself the opportunity to take her in. I couldn't help but wonder what had actually happened to her. It was clear this was exactly where she belonged. The ice was hers and no one else's.

I couldn't help myself and I couldn't look away.

There was something about her—something ethereal. Something godly. She didn't seem to care about anyone else that was skating. She was in her own world, listening to the tune of her blades cutting through the ice.

"I would suggest you stop wherever your thoughts are going now, Mac," Lincoln said with his voice low. "She's the coach's daughter. You know that automatically makes her off-limits."

I looked back at him with a scowl. "I don't know what you're even talking about. I was just watching her skate."

Lincoln pursed his lips. "I know that look, bro. She caught your attention."

"Is that a bad thing?"

He raised his eyebrows. "Uh, yeah. It is when her father is our coach."

Fuck, he was right. I couldn't get any ideas. She was untouchable. Even if I found myself sparked with intrigue, I couldn't let my mind wander. I couldn't explore any of that. Relationships weren't something I was interested in. I was merely looking for a good time with anyone who caught my eye. It would be a recipe for disaster. She was someone I couldn't pursue because I knew it would blow up in my face—and the last thing I needed was a scandal.

I didn't need to be on our coach's shit list for any reason.

Especially if he caught me looking at his daughter.

"I was just watching her, Linc. Nothing more than that."

He snorted. "Sure. Just remember that the next time your eyes start to wander in the wrong direction. Don't fuck your career up because your dick is curious."

I cut my eyes at him, stifling a laugh. "I'm not that stupid."

He didn't look convinced. "Let's hope not."

CHAPTER TWO
JULIETTE

I was the last one off the ice after the family skate had ended and I took a seat on one of the benches along the hallway as I undid the laces of my skates. It wasn't often that I had the opportunity to skate on professional ice and when my father invited my mother and me, I wasn't about to turn that down. The fact that I didn't play anymore didn't change anything, really, except my mindset on actually playing.

Two years ago, during my senior year of college, I got into a car accident and messed up my leg. It wasn't bad enough that I couldn't skate anymore, but it was too risky to continue playing the caliber of hockey I was headed toward. Now, my time on the ice was spent helping coach some of the kids at our local rink. I couldn't even bring myself to play in an adult league.

If I couldn't play the way I used to, I didn't even want to play at all.

I was following more in my father's footsteps and leading others on the ice instead of living out my own dreams. They were taken away from me a lot sooner than I had imagined it would happen.

After putting on my skate guards, I stood up and slid my feet into my sneakers and tucked them under my arm as I headed down the hallway. It was empty and there wasn't a single soul in sight. My father's office was the first stop I made and I was expecting to see my mother and him inside, but the lights were turned off and the door was shut.

I checked in the family room and found it empty too. It was like everyone had vanished from the arena completely. The next two rooms that I checked were the same. Not paying attention, I moved to another door and pushed it open. It was the last one that I hadn't looked inside and if my parents weren't in here, then they had to have been outside waiting.

As I stepped inside, the lights were on and I realized I had walked into the locker room. My feet froze and I glanced around, noticing I was alone. Someone must have forgotten to turn the lights off after they left. Casting a nervous glance over my shoulder, I took another step and began to walk around the perimeter of the room, avoiding the Vipers' logo in the center of the floor.

My eyes traveled over the names and all of the players' gear. I couldn't help but feel envious, knowing that I could have had a similar future on a professional women's team if I wouldn't have gotten into that damn car accident. I wasn't even driving… I was merely a passenger who stupidly got into a car with someone who had been drinking. When Tate veered off the road and hit the tree, the majority of the impact was on my side.

I was lost in my own thoughts with the painful reminders wrapping around my throat like a vise grip. My heart constricted and I felt the weight of my own despair pressing on my rib cage. You would think two years would be enough time to get past something like that, but I lived with those thoughts every day. It was hard to get past something that completely changed the trajectory of your life.

"Are you lost?"

I jumped at the sound of his voice. Low and husky. It abruptly ripped me out of my head and I spun on my heel to face the stranger who had crept up on me.

As I turned in his direction, heat instantly crept up my neck and spread across my face. He was shirtless, his body damp from the shower he just took and a towel secured around his waist as he leaned against the doorway. I couldn't help myself as my eyes traveled across the planes of his body, trailing over the lines of his muscles. His hair was dark, hanging just above his eyebrows with droplets of water falling onto his temples.

"I—uh—I was just looking for my father," I choked out the words as I forced my gaze to meet his. His crystal blue eyes were burning holes through my own with a smirk situated on his lips.

He pushed away from the doorjamb and took a few steps closer to me. "Ah, you're Coach Anderson's daughter, aren't you?"

I narrowed my eyes as I stared at him. I wanted to smack the stupid cocky grin from his face. He was looking at me the same way I had seen plenty of other guys look at me. There was a burning curiosity in those blue eyes of his and I needed to extinguish the fire before it burned deeper.

"I am, and you are?"

He raked his hand through his hair, messing up the damp curls. "Mac Sullivan."

I pursed my lips and hummed as I cocked my head to the side. "That's not a familiar name to me, I'm sorry. You must not be important enough for my father to ever mention your name."

It was a lie, but I wasn't about to show my cards. He didn't need to know that my father spoke highly of him and the high hopes he had for him on the team. This man didn't need me to feed his ego when clearly he could feed it himself.

His expression didn't falter. If anything, he grew more amused and raised an eyebrow as he studied me for a moment. "Fair enough," he said with a shrug of indifference. "As you can see, your father isn't here. It's just me."

"I've gathered that much."

Mac stood where he was and his eyes followed me as I took a step toward the door. "I saw you out on the ice. Rumor has it you used to play hockey. What happened?"

My brows furrowed, my spine straightening as I stopped mid-step. I swallowed roughly over the lump that formed in my throat. It wasn't something that I enjoyed talking about and I wasn't about to discuss it with someone who was living the dream I envisioned for myself. "It doesn't matter."

"Sure it does," he said matter-of-factly. "I saw you out there. It's clear that you have talent. What's keeping you from playing?"

"I don't think that's any of your business," I clipped as my gaze hardened on his. "I coach youth hockey now. That's enough for me."

He didn't look convinced. "Sorry for asking. I'll remember in the future that it's a touchy subject."

I rolled my eyes. "There won't be any future conversations between us."

"Why's that?"

He was beginning to grate on my damn nerves. "I know your type and I'm not interested. I grew up in a hockey rink, I know how guys like you operate. Trust me… anything you're about to say or try has already been done before, so just save it for one of the girls that worships you like you're a hockey god and falls at your feet like an idiot."

"Damn, are you this mean to everyone you meet?"

He laughed it off and shook his head. "For the record, I never said I was interested. I was merely making polite conversation and figured I'd see you around here again sometime."

I ignored his question and his statement about not being interested. "That's doubtful."

"I'm not your enemy, you know," he said softly as he closed the distance between us. His lips parted and a soft breath escaped him. "It doesn't hurt to be nice to people."

I stared at him for two heartbeats as his words swirled around in my head. He was insignificant in my life. Just another player on the team my father coached. He'd probably end up being traded in a season or two and I'd never hear of him again except while watching highlights on TV.

"I need to go find my father."

Mac pursed his lips and nodded. "He's out in the parking lot."

"Why didn't you tell me that when I first walked in here?" I demanded, feeling the irritation prickle my skin. Moving to Orchid City was my mother's idea. I was content back in our hometown in Maine. She insisted I move here to be closer to my family and I agreed when I was able to get a job at the local hospital.

The corners of his lips twitched. "Because then I wouldn't have had the opportunity to talk to you."

I snorted. "Was it everything you imagined it would be?"

He smiled, flashing his straight white teeth. "Oh, it exceeded my expectations."

"Glad to hear it," I said with a snarky tone as I finally turned away from him. The last thing I needed was someone like Mac Sullivan under my skin. Hockey players weren't my type, especially cocky ones who were overly sure of themselves like him. The air sizzled between us and the tension was palpable. My feet carried me closer to the door as I put as much distance between us as possible.

"Hey," Mac called out after me as I reached for the door. "I didn't get your name…"

I didn't chance a glance back in his direction. I didn't need to see his perfect white smile and chiseled jaw. I didn't need those clear blue eyes searching mine.

"Because I didn't tell you and you don't need to know it."

CHAPTER THREE
MAC

It was late at night by the time I got back to my condo building. After the game, a few of us went and got drinks before going our separate ways. I had a bit of a buzz, but I wasn't drunk. As the elevator reached my floor and I stepped out, I came to a halt, my feet unmoving as I stared down the hall. Just across from my door was someone sitting outside of the other condo. Her dark hair was pulled up in a messy bun on top of her head and she was sitting cross-legged with her back against the door. My eyebrows scrunched in confusion, but I slowly began to approach.

And then I realized who it was.

Coach Anderson's daughter.

"Hey," I said softly as I stopped directly in front of her. She caught me off guard. I hadn't seen her since the family skate... and I wasn't expecting to find her in the hallway of my condo building. "Whatcha doing down there?"

She lifted her head abruptly, her eyes widening as they met mine in a rush. "You again. What are you doing here?"

A chuckle escaped me and I pointed to the door behind me. "I live here. What exactly are you doing here, and why are you sitting on the floor?"

"Shit," she murmured and shook her head before tilting it back to lean against the door. "I just moved in, like, two days ago and I already locked myself out."

"Do I even want to ask how you managed to do that?"

She let out a sigh and straightened her head as she looked back at me. "I'd rather you didn't."

"You don't have a spare key anywhere?"

She shook her head. "I called the property manager. They're supposed to be sending someone out within the next few hours."

I glanced at the watch on my wrist. "It's already after midnight."

"Yeah, I know," she said as her shoulders sagged with slight defeat. "It's fine. I'm the one who locked myself out, so I don't mind waiting for them."

I studied her for a moment as she picked at her cuticles. "Come hang out at my place until they come."

She raised an eyebrow at me. "I appreciate the offer, but I'm fine waiting here."

I shrugged and dropped down onto the floor across

from her. If she wanted to be stubborn, two could play that game.

"What are you doing?"

A smirk pulled on my lips and I blinked at her. "Waiting with you. Who knows who the hell they're sending here in the middle of the night. I'll stay until you're in your condo safely."

"You don't have to do that," she said softly as warmth flooded her eyes.

My smirk turned into a smile and I nodded. "I know, but if you don't want to come and wait at my place, then I'll stay out here."

She stared at me for a moment as if she were weighing the options. I didn't want her sitting out in the hallway waiting for some stranger to show up. I knew I was equally a stranger to her, but I was the safer option. I just wanted her to have somewhere to sit instead of the dirty floor in the hallway.

"Fine, I'll come to your place," she said after the silence stretched between us. She climbed to her feet and I followed suit. "But don't get any ideas."

I couldn't help but laugh as I turned and slid the key into the lock of my door. "I would never."

She snorted as I unlocked the door.

I paused. "Are you afraid of dogs?"

She shook her head at me. "No, why?"

A smile lifted my lips as I opened the door for her. I moved out of the way, motioning for her to go ahead inside just as Thor came running toward us.

"Thor, sit," I commanded and he dropped to his bottom, his tongue hanging out as his tail beat against his sides. "This is Thor. He's harmless."

She stepped past me and I caught the floral scent of her perfume. It invaded my senses, momentarily freezing my mind. I watched as she crouched down in front of my dog, murmuring something to him as she pet his head. Slowly, she stood back up and her eyes met mine. She waited for me to lead the way through my condo and I had to snap myself out of my stupor.

"Do you want anything to drink?" I asked her as we stepped into the kitchen with Thor running past us.

"Sure," she said with a shrug of indifference. "Do you have any wine?"

"White or red?"

She smiled quickly before it fell away from her lips. "Red, please."

She stood off to the side, leaning against the counter as I grabbed a bottle of wine and two glasses and began to pour the liquid into them. I slowly approached her, careful not to get too close as I handed one to her.

"Are you ever going to tell me your name?"

Her gaze held mine as she lifted her glass to her lips and slowly took a sip. I watched the way her throat moved as she swallowed. Her tongue darted out, licking her lips as she continued to stare at me. "Juliette."

"Juliette," I said softly, tasting her name on my tongue as I held my hand out to her. She eyed me skeptically before sliding her palm against mine. "It's a pleasure to officially meet you."

She didn't agree with me, but she also didn't disagree, so I was willing to take that as a win. Juliette sipped her wine again as she slowly took in my condo. It was an open floor plan, with the dining room, kitchen, and living room all bleeding into one space. "Your place is... nice."

I tilted my head to the side, my lips lifting. "Was that a compliment?"

Juliette raised an eyebrow and pursed her lips. "It was an observation, nothing more."

"I don't know. That sounded a lot like a compliment."

"Well, perhaps you need to have your hearing or comprehension skills checked." She rolled her eyes at me. "So, you guys won tonight?"

I nodded. "Did you watch the game?"

Juliette stared at me with something unreadable in her gaze. "No."

That was it. No offering or explanation. Just a flat-out no. Clearly, I had lost all ability to read a room properly and decided no wasn't a good enough answer.

"How did you know we won?"

She took another sip of her wine. "You seem to be in a good mood, so it was just a guess."

I couldn't help my curiosity when it came to her. She was a mystery, like a code I needed to crack. She appeared confident and independent, but there was something underneath the mask she wore. It was clear she didn't care for hockey players… or perhaps it was just me in particular. She was a challenge.

And I never walked away from a challenge.

"It was a good guess," I agreed with her as I walked out of the kitchen and into the living room. Much to my surprise, she followed after me and sat down on the couch, putting enough distance between us after I took a seat. Thor sat down beside her, resting his head in her lap as she slowly stroked the fur on top of his snout. I studied her for a moment. I liked how she looked in my space. Clearly my dog was infatuated with her. "What brings you to Orchid City? You're not from around here, right?"

She shook her head. "No, I'm from Maine originally. My mother insisted I move down here since they weren't planning on coming back north anytime soon." She paused and shrugged. "A change of scenery never hurts. I was able to interview and get a job at Orchid City Hospital."

Another unexpected response from Juliette. I wanted to ask her about hockey. I knew she had some kind of an accident in college, but I saw the way she skated. I also knew it was potentially a sensitive topic and the last thing I wanted to do was scare her away this early. She already had the look of a frightened animal. She acted like she might flee at any given moment.

I'd ask her about it one day, but today wasn't that day.

"What do you do?"

Juliette sighed. "I'm a marketing specialist for the hospital and I coach youth hockey in my free time. I would ask what you do, but I already know the answer to that."

I laughed softly in an attempt to get her to crack a smile, but it was like pulling teeth trying to get through her cold exterior. I figured as long as I could keep her talking, I was in safe territory. As long as I kept it superficial and not prying. "Do you like it there?"

Her lips moved, lifting upward in the slightest bit. "No idea," she said with a lilt in her voice. "My first day is tomorrow." She paused and looked at the watch on her wrist. "Actually, my first day is in seven hours, so ask me again after that."

"Oh shit," I murmured as I looked at the time on my phone. It was a little after midnight. "We need to get you back into your condo. You need to get some sleep before your big day tomorrow."

She laughed softly, the sound fleeting. "Please. It's my first day at work, not my first day of kindergarten."

"Hey, don't be dismissive. It's still a big thing."

Juliette looked amused for a beat and her eyes shimmered as she stared back at me. Her phone began to vibrate and she pulled it out from the pocket of her hoodie. "It's the property manager. They must be here."

I let out a sigh of relief for her. I didn't really know her and I shouldn't have cared about her getting sleep, but I couldn't help myself. Juliette rose to her feet and walked into the kitchen as she answered the call. She wasn't on the phone long before she called my name from where she was, pulling me out of my own thoughts.

"Thanks for letting me hang out here," she said softly as I walked into the kitchen where she was standing. She had set her glass of wine by the sink and was already making her way toward the door. She gave Thor a final pat on the head before leaving him too.

"You're more than welcome to hang out here anytime you lock yourself out," I told her as I followed behind her.

"Hopefully that doesn't happen again," she muttered as she reached for the door. Her eyebrows pinched together when I grabbed the handle and pulled the door open wider. "What are you doing?"

I tilted my chin down to meet her gaze. "Coming with you."

"You don't have to do that," she said as she straightened her spine.

"I know I don't." I didn't know who the hell brought a key here for her, but I wasn't going to let her go out to meet this stranger by herself. There wasn't a part of me that doubted Juliette's ability to take care of herself, but at that moment her safety was my priority. I needed to know for myself that she got into her condo without any issues and without someone else forcing their way in with her.

She let out a sigh and shook her head before turning away from me. She walked across the hall to her door where a younger guy was waiting with a key. "Are you Juliette Anderson?" he asked her.

"I am. Thank you for coming out so late at night."

The guy nodded. "It's not a problem, although I'd recommend getting a spare key made and either giving it to someone or storing it somewhere."

Juliette didn't respond and I stood behind her, crossing my arms over my chest as he unlocked her door for her and pushed it open. Soft music was playing from somewhere inside her condo and it must have been on from before she locked herself out earlier.

The guy glanced at me with a questioning look and I simply stared back at him with my jaw set. He didn't say anything to me before looking back to Juliette to tell her to have a good night. I huffed under my breath and glared at the back of his head as he walked back down the hall toward the elevator.

Juliette turned back around to look at me. "Well, thanks again," she said softly, almost like she wasn't sure what to say. Like she was nervous.

I relaxed under her gaze and unfolded my arms before tucking my hands into the front pockets of my pants. "I'm right across the hall if you ever need anything," I offered with a smile. "Good luck with your first day of kindergarten tomorrow."

She smiled. Like really smiled. The kind of smile that lights up someone's face and spreads onto your own. My heart skipped a beat in my chest.

"Good night, Mac," she said as she quickly put her guard back in place.

The smile on my own lips didn't falter. "Good night, Juliette."

I walked back to my own door, my footsteps deliberately slow as I waited for her to step into her condo. I listened to the sound of the door shutting and the locks clicking before I went back into my own place.

I knew I needed to keep my distance from her. She was technically off-limits. There were unspoken rules in place, ones that I was expected to follow if I didn't want to fuck up my career.

Unfortunately for me, I never was good at following rules.

CHAPTER FOUR
JULIETTE

The next morning came quickly. I spent the entire night tossing and turning, mainly from the anxiety of starting a new job, but there was also something else lingering in my subconscious. Those damn blue eyes that wouldn't stop staring at me last night. Mac Sullivan was the last thing I needed in my life. Hockey players were not my type. *He* was not my type.

My brain needed to get its shit together. He was nice to me last night and that was it. It could never be anything more than that. I needed to focus on my own life and I wasn't going to let some overly confident hockey player get in the way of that.

I needed to erase Mac from my mind as quickly as he had entered it.

Pushing the lingering thoughts and the tiredness from my foggy head, I went through the motions of getting ready before leaving my condo. I was sure to bring my keys this time because the last thing I needed was a repeat of last night. If I were smart, I would keep my distance from my neighbor across the hall.

After getting ready, I headed down to my car. It was early and the sun was just barely cresting the horizon as I drove through the city to the hospital. It was only a twenty-minute drive and I was thankful for finding a place to live that didn't have a long commute.

Today was just my first day of orientation. I had to go through a few days of learning the systems and the hospital's policies before starting training with the actual marketing department. When I walked into the room, there were six different places set with packets of information. Since it was orientation day for the hospital, there were going to be other new hires from different departments with me today.

I was the first one there, so I took a seat at one of the tables at the front of the room. It wasn't long before everyone else started to arrive and the seat next to me was occupied. I glanced over at my table mate as she sat down with a bright smile.

"Hi!" she greeted in a cheerful voice. I felt like I was half asleep, while she looked like she had been awake for four hours already. "I'm Lyla."

I stifled a yawn. She was too kind for me to be rude, even if I wasn't exactly a morning person. "Hey. I'm Juliette."

Lyla's blonde hair was pulled back in a ponytail

without a single hair out of place. She looked to be in her mid-twenties and was dressed in scrubs. I scanned her for a moment for a name tag but couldn't find one. She didn't notice as she took a sip of her coffee and glanced around the room.

"What unit are you going to be working in?" she asked me as her gaze met mine once again.

"I'm actually not a nurse. I'll be in the marketing department."

Her face lit up and excitement slid across her expression. "No way, me too! How cool," she said before the smile fell from her face. "Sorry, I know I can be a little much sometimes. I just moved here recently and I don't know anyone." She laughed nervously.

I stared at her for a moment, instantly feeling regret for the coldness I had been exuding. It was easy for me to give off the vibe and appearance that I didn't care. Especially in the morning when I slept terribly the night before. This poor girl was simply excited at the possibility of making a new friend, and here I was making her feel insecure about being authentic.

"Don't ever apologize for something like that. You never owe anyone an apology for being yourself." I paused for a moment, my face softening as I offered her a warm smile in return. "I just moved here too, so I know exactly how you are feeling."

Lyla let out a sigh of relief. "It's so hard meeting people and making friends as an adult. I only lived an hour away but I figured moving to the city would make things easier with work. I didn't realize how lonely it would be here."

I didn't come here looking for a new friend, but Lyla was right. It was incredibly isolating and lonely. The closest thing I had to a friend was my neighbor across the hall, and there was a part of me that couldn't stand him. He also wasn't a friend—just merely an acquaintance I had contact with.

"Well, you know what? We will tackle that obstacle together then."

Her eyes widened. "Really? I mean, I don't want you to feel like we have to be friends or anything."

"Lyla, just stop," I told her, shaking my head. "We're friends now, so I'm going to be upfront with you. Stop apologizing to me and making assumptions. If I didn't want to be your friend, I wouldn't."

This poor girl severely lacked confidence. I didn't know who told her she was too much before, but whoever they were, they were an asshole.

"Okay, okay," she said as she laughed softly. The other seats in the room had since filled in with the other new hires, and Lyla and I both turned to the front of the room as the man leading our orientation walked in.

I yawned as he wasted no time diving straight into the hospital's policies. Lyla had her notebook flipped open and was eagerly following along.

This was going to be a long day.

After a full day of listening to the policies and going over all of the paperwork, I was finally free. Although, I had to come back tomorrow to head into the next phase of orientation. There was a part of me that didn't want to go back. As much as I enjoyed marketing, I wanted more from life. I wanted something that I was passionate about, not just a mindless job to pay the bills.

I wanted hockey, but that wasn't an option. At least, not in the capacity that I wanted it to be.

Lyla was sure to give me her number before I walked out of the building. We parted ways with the promise of making plans soon and seeing each other bright and early the next day. I didn't know where her energy came from because she barely looked exhausted when the day was over.

The elevator took me up to my floor and my feet felt heavy as I stepped into the hall. I was ready for a glass of wine, a bath, and a good book to get lost in. Just as I was reaching my door, I heard a sound behind me. I turned around without even thinking about it.

Mac's gaze met mine from across the hall as he stepped out of his condo with another guy following behind him. I watched his face transform from annoyed to amused, the creases falling away from his forehead as his eyes softened and a smile crept onto his lips.

"Hey you," he said slowly, his voice warm and welcoming. "How was your first day of school?"

My mouth twitched and I snorted. "It really has me second-guessing my life choices."

A touch of concern washed over his expression and he tilted his head to the side. I watched him for a moment as his lips parted like he wanted to say something, but he quickly shut them as his friend stepped beside him.

"You're Juliette, right? Coach Anderson's daughter?"

As if the day wasn't taxing enough, that question deflated me completely. I had always lived in my father's shadow and it was no different here. I was stupid to think I would be known for anything other than being the coach's daughter.

A sigh escaped me and I nodded. "Lincoln Matthews."

He was much more attractive up close, but he wasn't Mac. My body tensed at the thought. I needed those thoughts to be extinguished immediately.

His green eyes narrowed for a moment as he smirked. "You know who I am?"

I rolled my eyes. "I know who all of you are."

Mac raised a questioning brow at me and I shrugged. Mischief danced in his blue eyes, but he didn't touch the subject of me denying knowing who he was when we first met. I brushed off the unwanted thoughts of him and straightened my spine.

"You should come out with us," Lincoln offered with a wink. I watched Mac from the corner of my eye as his body instantly went rigid.

"I'd rather not," I told him in a bored tone as I

finally unlocked my door and turned the handle. I stepped past the threshold, turning to look at the two men across from me once more, but my eyes met Mac's instead. "Try to stay out of trouble tonight. It would be a shame if either of you messed up your careers by doing something stupid and careless."

Lincoln looked confused and Mac looked pissed.

I shut the door without another word and locked it behind me.

Moving here was definitely a mistake.

CHAPTER FIVE
MAC

"So, are we going to talk about whatever the hell that was?" Lincoln questioned me as we climbed into his car. I glanced over at him, meeting his green eyes before I shook my head.

"Nope."

Lincoln rolled his eyes as he started the engine and backed his car out of the parking spot. "When were you going to tell me she moved in across the hall from you?"

I shrugged. "It wasn't worth mentioning. She moved in a couple days ago. There's not much else to say about it." I paused, mulling over how much information I was willing to spill. "We've only seen each other in passing."

"Hm," he hummed, merging into rush-hour traffic. "Whatever that was between the two of you definitely looked a little more than that, but I'll let it go—for now."

I stared straight ahead, looking out the windshield without giving anything away through my expression. "You really want to talk about me after you just invited her to come out with us?"

Lincoln laughed out loud and shook his head at me. "She said no. And I only asked because I wanted to see how you would react."

"A test?" I asked him with irritation heating my blood. "Really?"

He shrugged with indifference and flashed me a look of innocence as he pulled into the parking lot at the end of the pier. "Don't take it personally, Sullivan. I just don't want to see you get into any trouble for fucking Anderson's daughter."

"Number one," I told him as I climbed out of his car. "I'm not fucking her. Number two. If I was, I wouldn't get caught doing it."

The words tasted bitter on my tongue as soon as they left my mouth. It was mainly to get Lincoln off my back, but I couldn't help but internally cringe as I played them over in my head again. It made me sound like I was a pig. If Juliette had heard me speak those words, I was certain she'd never talk to me again.

I wouldn't blame her. It was a fucked-up thing to say, but it worked.

Lincoln chuckled and fell into step beside me as we headed toward the pier. "I knew you were smart."

I pushed him away from me, listening to the ocean breeze carrying his laughter as we walked up to the bar. Nico and Wes were already there waiting for us. They both turned to look at Lincoln and I as we sat down next to them.

"Look who finally decided to show up," Wes said with his eyebrows raised. "Better late than never, I suppose."

"Are you really one to talk when you're late to everything?" Nico challenged him.

I laughed and nodded at Nico before looking back at Wes. "The only reason you're on time is because Nico brought you here."

"Hey, this isn't attack Wes time," he said, feigning innocence as he raised his hands in the air. "Sit down and drink up. First round's on me."

Lincoln didn't hesitate to grab the drink the bartender slid in front of him. "You don't have to tell me twice."

"What took you guys so long, though?" Wes questioned us, unable to keep his curiosity to himself. He was always nosy and never hesitated to probe and ask questions.

I grabbed my drink and swallowed a mouthful as I ignored his question, hoping Lincoln would do the same. He didn't, and I avoided eye contact with the three of them.

"We ran into Mac's new neighbor in the hall. Want to tell them who it is?"

Shaking my head, I stared up at one of the TVs hanging above the bar. I could feel Wes and Nico staring at me, but I wasn't going to take the bait. Lincoln was going to tell them anyway and it was better if I just kept my mouth shut.

"Coach Anderson's daughter," Lincoln said after leaving them in suspense for a moment. "She moved into the condo across the hall from Mac."

"No way," Wes said with a lilt of laughter in his voice at the same time Nico spoke sternly.

"No, Mac."

I slowly turned my head to look past Wes, and directly at Nico. "Excuse me?"

I didn't know how the hell he became the dad of our group, but it was really fucking irritating sometimes. He was the last one to be lecturing anyone after he ended up with one of the photographers from our team who got fired because of their relationship.

"You know you can't even entertain any thoughts about her."

My brows furrowed. "Who said I was even thinking about her?"

"Why was it such a big deal that you didn't want to tell us who your new neighbor was?" He pursed his lips. "Seems suspicious that you casually avoided engaging in the conversation then."

"Because there's nothing to talk about," I told him with a bite in my tone.

Nico gave me a look that said he didn't believe a single word I was saying. I was clearly a liar, because yes, I had thought about her. But I also knew Juliette Anderson was off-limits and she obviously didn't even like me.

"She came over the other night because she was locked out of her condo. That was it."

"Oh shit," Wes said with amusement. "You said there was nothing to talk about, yet you've already hung out with her."

"I didn't hang out with her. She just came over for a little while until the property manager came to let her back into her place," I explained, even though I didn't owe either of them an explanation.

Nico's expression softened. "Listen, I'm not saying any of this to be a dick. This is all coming from a place of experience." He paused for a moment, taking a sip of his drink. "You don't want to go there, man. She's our coach's daughter. If they find out, you'll be off the team without a second thought."

"Oh my god," I groaned, running my hand down my face. "She literally moved in across the hall. Please stop acting like I'm doing something bad by being nice to her."

"That's how it always starts out, my dude," Wes said with a smirk. It was like he and Nico were playing good cop and bad cop. Wes was always the good cop. Nico was the hard-ass through and through. "You start off being nice, next thing you know, you're waking up and she's walking around your condo wearing your t-shirt."

I glared at him. "Please just shut the fuck up."

"Hold up," Lincoln finally chimed in. "Stop acting like Sullivan is a dumbass. He's a grown man, he can make his own decisions. There's nothing going on between the two of them, so stop with the third degree, Cirone."

Turning to look at Lincoln, I silently thanked him for jumping on my side. This was typical with Nico and sometimes he needed to be knocked down a peg or two.

"Plus, you jeopardized your girl's entire career after you got involved with her," Lincoln reminded him with an eyebrow raised.

Nico looked between the two of us and Wes pulled out his phone as he dipped out of the conversation. He hated confrontation and had added enough fuel to the fire. A sigh escaped Nico and his nostrils flared as he subtly shook his head.

"Okay, my bad," he said with a solemn expression. There was a touch of regret in his eyes. "I shouldn't have jumped down your throat about it. I just know how these kinds of things can go and we can't afford to lose you on the team."

I stared at him for a second as he gave me an apologetic look. I couldn't fault him for acting like our dad sometimes. He had to step into that role for his sister after his mother passed away and his father became vacant. It was in his nature and he protected the people he was close to—even if it came off as abrasive and felt like he was being an asshole.

A smile pulled on my lips. "Aww. So, what you're really saying is, you don't want to see them get rid of me? You want me around."

Nico rolled his eyes but smiled back. "Yes, you fucking idiot." He shook his head again. "Just don't do anything dumb. And if you do, for the love of God, protect yourself and don't get into any trouble."

"Look at this softie," Wes crooned as he lightly punched Nico in the bicep. "You really do care, don't you?"

Laughter erupted between the four of us and I tilted my head as I looked back at Nico. "Don't worry. I'm pretty positive she can't stand me, so there's no chance of anything happening."

Nico didn't look convinced, but he didn't touch back on the subject as Lincoln swiftly turned the conversation away from Juliette. The four of us fell into our typical hockey talk before shifting into life stuff. It was mainly Wes and Nico talking since Lincoln and I were the two who were still single and didn't have girlfriends that we had stuff going on with.

We drank well into the night before we all ended up too drunk to drive. Wes's girlfriend Charlotte came and picked both of us up, while Nico's girlfriend Harper picked him up. Lincoln lived closer to Nico and Harper, so she was giving him a ride home too. We would all just have to come back to the pier the next day to get our cars.

Charlotte was polite and nice, as she always was, laughing at Wes and I as we both drunkenly sang along to some pop song on the radio. Wes stared at her, belting the words as he reached out and touched the side of her face. I slowly stopped singing and watched both of them, feeling a twinge of jealousy. Sober me didn't want what they had, but drunk me did.

Turning my head, I looked out the window to distract myself from them just as Charlotte pulled up in front of my condo building. Wes was still singing but she turned back to look at me.

"Are you okay to get in by yourself, Mac?"

I gave her a crooked smile. "Yes, mother. I will be fine."

She rolled her eyes and laughed softly. "Get out of my damn car."

"Yeah, get lost, Sullivan," Wes slurred as he chuckled and slid his hand onto Charlotte's thigh. "I'm ready for Charlotte to take me home so I can strip her naked and—"

"That's enough, pretty boy," she cut him off as she smiled at him and shook her head as she patted his cheek.

I didn't need any more encouragement and climbed out of the car as if it were on fire. Wes had no problem with PDA and when he got drunk, I almost felt bad for

Charlotte. She took him in stride and had a fiery side that wouldn't hesitate to put him in his place.

"Thanks for the ride, Charlie," I told her before shutting the door. Throwing a wave over my shoulder, I stepped up to the front door and punched in my code to get into the building. Charlotte pulled the car away from the curb as I disappeared inside.

After stumbling through the lobby, I slipped into the mail room and emptied out the contents from inside my box. There was a cardboard box inside that I grabbed, even though I didn't remember ordering anything. I leaned against the wall in the elevator as I took it up to my floor, feeling the alcohol in my system weighing me down. My eyelids were growing heavier by the second and my legs were a resemblance of Jell-O.

Somehow I managed to get inside my condo, dropping my mail onto the counter before fetching a glass of water. I swiftly drained the cup and eyed the small package with my things. Picking it up, I pulled the tab off the cardboard and ripped it open. A book dropped out of it and landed in front of me. Confusion washed over me and my eyebrows scrunched as I picked it up. It was a romance novel.

What the hell? There was no reason I would order a book. I was borderline illiterate.

Picking up the packaging, I squinted my eyes as I tried to read the mailing label. The words blurred together a bit, undoubtedly from the alcohol, but I could make out the name of who it was addressed to.

Juliette Anderson.

She was the one who had ordered the book. It ended up in my mailbox as a mistake and I opened it without even realizing it wasn't my package. I dropped the cardboard onto the floor and picked the book up again as I inspected it.

A smirk slowly pulled on my lips. I knew I needed to keep my distance from Juliette, but now I had a reason to talk to her. As I fanned through the pages, I decided I wasn't going to give the book to her… not yet, at least.

I was going to read it first and then she could have it.

Maybe I could learn a thing or two about her from what she liked to read.

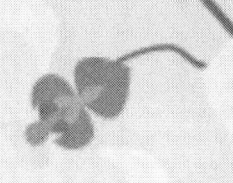

CHAPTER SIX
JULIETTE

Skating backward, I leaned back against the net as I watched the six-year-olds start their scrimmage game. A smile pulled on my lips as Chase, one of the other coaches, tossed the puck onto the ice. Two of the kids instantly fell down while another two battled over the puck. The other four kids were waiting for something to happen. It was entertaining watching them all, considering most of them were new to the sport and were still learning the game.

When I moved to Orchid City, my father told me about a youth program at one of the local rinks. They were in need of coaches and with the background I had, they didn't even need to know anything else about me. It wasn't a paid position, just volunteering, but it was enough for me.

Dante, the hockey director, had told me they were potentially going to open a paid position for a youth development coordinator and I was the first on their list for the spot, as long as I proved myself this season. I desperately wanted it—no, I *needed* it.

A career in hockey was always my dream. Having to fall back on my backup plan and work as a marketing specialist was something I never actually imagined having to do. My ego took a hit and so did my heart. Marketing wasn't what I wanted to do with my life, but if I wanted to live, I had no choice at this point. I worked hard for that degree, even if I never planned on using it.

If I really wanted to, I could have moved in with my parents and lived off the money they had in a trust for me. After I turned eighteen, I could access the funds they spent years saving for me. While my father played hockey professionally, my parents were smart with their finances. My mom didn't give up her own dreams and still went on to be a pediatrician.

They made it work. If anything, watching both of them instilled a lot of my own core values. And even though I never had to want for anything while I was growing up, I wanted independence. I didn't want to live off my parents, and I sure as hell didn't want to live off of anyone else's money either.

I was fortunate enough that I went to college on a full-ride scholarship. I didn't touch the money my parents had saved for me until I moved to Orchid City. I tapped into some of it to use as a down payment on the condo I bought. In a way, it was an impulsive decision. I didn't know whether or not I would plan to stay here, but my parents were always big on building assets.

Even if I decided Orchid City wasn't the place for me, I could just rent out the condo instead.

And there was a large part of me that was considering whether or not this was where I belonged.

I wanted to go back up north, back to everything I knew. There were so many more hockey rinks back home. So many more opportunities. Not to mention I could count the friends I had made here on one finger.

After practice ended, I headed into the locker room and helped one of the little ones untie their skates while she waited for her parents to come in and help. She tilted her head back at me, peering up at me with honey brown eyes through the cage of her helmet.

"Coach Jules," she said softly before glancing around at her teammates in the locker room. She lowered her voice to almost a whisper, as if she didn't want anyone else to hear her. "I don't think I'm very good at this."

I tilted my head to the side, my brow furrowing. "Sydney, you're six. I needed help tying my skates until I was almost ten—and even then, I didn't do a very good job."

"Not my skates." She frowned and shook her head. "Hockey. I'm not very good."

My heart clenched as I heard the sadness in her voice and I slid the blade protectors over her skates before setting them down beside her. Reaching for the straps of her helmet, I unsnapped them and undid her chin strap. Sydney pulled her helmet from her head and cradled it in her lap as she looked back up at me through her thick lashes.

Bending my knees, I crouched back down in front of her. "You're just getting started, Syd. There aren't many kids that are very good at hockey this young. I promise if you keep trying, you'll get better."

"But you're really good."

A soft laugh escaped me. "I've been playing hockey for a really long time. I would hope to be good by now." She still didn't look convinced even though she cracked a small smile. "Can I tell you a secret?"

She nodded as she chewed on her bottom lip.

"When I was twelve, I tried out for this one team and I didn't make it."

A confused look washed over her expression. "What do you mean?"

"I tried out for the team and they told me no. They told me that I wasn't good enough to play with that team." It wasn't a lie. I was shooting for the AA team and ended up being bumped down to A instead.

"So what did you do?"

I smiled at her. "I didn't give up. I played on a different team and I played even harder. I practiced all the time, so when tryouts came around for the next season I would be good enough."

Sydney smiled back at me, her lips curving upward

as her eyes brightened with hope. "I can do it. I can try harder and be better."

"As long as you're having fun, that is the most important thing."

"Oh, Coach Juliette," a feminine voice sounded from behind me. I stood up and turned around to meet Sydney's mother as she walked over to us. "Thank you so much for helping Sydney. I was stuck on a business call."

"No worries at all," I assured her with a nod. "Sydney is a great kid," I told her before winking at Syd. Her mother grinned and I stepped aside as she took my place in front of her daughter. I excused myself, telling all the kids they did great before making my way to the coaches' locker room.

It was empty when I stepped inside and took off my own skates. I couldn't help but see a bit of myself in Sydney. She had the drive and the determination. All she needed was confidence, but that would come over time. If she kept up with it, she could be a good player one day. There wasn't a doubt in my mind about that. She had grit and that would go a long way in an aggressive sport like hockey.

Practice for some of the older kids had already started by the time I was leaving the rink. After putting in a full day of work at the hospital and coming straight here for practice, I was exhausted by the time I reached my condo building. After letting myself in through the front, I stopped by the mail room to get my stuff. There was an email I saw this morning saying the book I had ordered was delivered yesterday, but I forgot to check for it earlier.

I opened my box and disappointment washed over me as I saw there were only two pieces of junk mail inside. Typically if there was a package delivered that didn't fit inside, they would leave a little slip for it to be picked up in the security office in the lobby. There wasn't even a slip in there. It was after hours, so I wouldn't be able to call the delivery company, but I would have to check tomorrow. There was always a chance of things getting lost in the mail, but I was really looking forward to reading my new book.

After closing the small door of my mailbox and locking it, I made my way to the elevator and leaned against the wall as I rode up to my floor. I loathed cooking. The only thing I couldn't burn was toast and pasta. I had no desire to make anything for myself and I had gotten into the bad habit of ordering out almost every single day.

Sometimes I wondered how the hell I fully functioned as an adult.

The elevator doors slid open and I stepped out into the hall. There were only two condos on each floor. I couldn't help myself as I glanced over at the door across from mine while I went to let myself into my place. I hadn't seen Mac today and there was a part of me that was glad. He was someone I wanted to avoid entirely... but my mind betrayed me. He infiltrated my thoughts when I desperately tried to pretend he didn't exist.

And just as I was unlocking my door, the universe decided it was the perfect time to test me.

Mac's door slowly opened and he stepped through the doorway, holding on to the leash attached to his dog. Thor spotted me from across the hall and his entire body began to wiggle as his tail started to wag. He let out a whine, pulling against Mac who was struggling to lock his door.

"Jesus, Thor, just hold on," he mumbled with frustration as he turned around. His eyes traveled across the hall, instantly colliding with mine. His expression softened and the corners of his lips lifted. He swiftly closed the distance between us with three long strides. "Well, hey there, neighbor. Now I see why Thor's so excited."

Heat crept across my cheeks and I ducked my head as I dropped my purse and backpack onto the floor and crouched down in front of Thor. "Hey you," I murmured as I pet his velvet soft head. "You're such a good boy, aren't you?"

"Sometimes I am," Mac said softly from where he was standing above us. I glanced up at him, narrowing my eyes as he smirked. "Oh, you meant the dog."

I patted Thor's head once more and slowly stood back up. "Yes. I was talking to him, not you." I snorted and rolled my eyes. "I don't care whether or not you're a good boy."

"I never wanted to be that dog as badly as I do right now."

I raised an eyebrow at him. "Something's seriously wrong with you."

"Maybe," he said with a shrug of indifference. His gaze was locked on mine and he took another step closer. "But if wanting your attention is wrong, then fuck ever being right."

The air left my lungs in a rush, my eyes widening as I stared back at him in shock. His words caught me off guard and I couldn't help but love the way they felt as the sound of his voice slid across my eardrums. Swallowing roughly, I leaned down and grabbed my bags before standing upright again. Pushing my shoulders back, I straightened my spine. I lifted my chin and shoved the feelings he elicited back into the box they belonged in.

The surprise washed away from my face and I gave him a blank stare. "You don't want my attention. I promise."

The muscle in Mac's jaw tightened, though his eyes never left mine. "I think I'll be the judge of that." He didn't take a step away from me and the hallway felt suffocating. "The harder you push, the more you're just reeling me in, Juliette."

My body finally responded as I forced my feet to move and take a step back from him. I didn't stop moving until I felt my door behind me. My lips parted but the only thing that escaped me was a shallow breath.

"I'll see you later, Juliette," he said softly before turning away from me. I watched as he led Thor to the elevator and only as the doors were about to close did his gaze meet mine once again.

And the heat burning in his irises was enough to set my entire soul on fire.

Mac Sullivan was someone I could not and would not get involved with.

But I had half a mind to consider the possibility of it…

CHAPTER SEVEN
MAC

Slowly turning the page, I closed the book in my hands, a slow smile creeping across my lips. Who knew that these romance novels had such dirty words written beneath the innocent-looking covers? Apparently Juliette did. Clicking the pen in my hand, I flipped the book back open and began to flip through the pages. She had no idea that I had her package, so I was going to leave a little surprise for her inside.

I went through all the pages again, scanning the text for the different parts that had my mind drifting to Juliette. I couldn't help but wonder what she liked—if the things she read were the things she fantasized about. She was confident, independent, and a fucking catch.

The first scene I ended up on was the first sex scene. The guy was taking her from behind on the balcony of his suite. His hand was tangled in her hair, exposing her neck as he pulled her head to her back. My pen scratched the surface of the paper as I etched my own little note in the margin.

I scribbled notes throughout the entire book before tucking it back in the small cardboard box it came in. There was a roll of packing tape in my kitchen and I closed the package and made sure it was secure before setting it back on my counter. Thor whined from where he was standing beside me and when I looked down at him, he barked.

"You want to go for a run?" I questioned him as I reached for his leash.

Thor barreled toward the door, his nails scratching against the wood floors as he slid to a stop and I laughed. He was so eager he almost fell down. His tongue hung out of his mouth and he panted while his tail wagged with excitement.

I realized I didn't have the proper attire on and Thor followed me through my condo as I took off my shirt and tossed it onto my bed. There were a pair of shorts folded on the bench at the end of my bed, so I slipped those on and grabbed my headphones. Thor continued to whine and his whole body moved side to side with his tail. Having him was both a blessing and a curse. He was like a bull in a china shop, knocking things over without realizing it.

"Let's go," I murmured to him as I slipped the harness around his neck and strapped it around his torso. I clipped the leash to it and stood upright as I placed my hand on the package. "Should we stop and see if our lovely neighbor is home?"

Thor's tongue hung out farther and he panted loudly. His face looked like he was smiling and his tail began to wag harder.

"Good idea," I said with a nod, even though he didn't actually say anything. I saw how she was with him. She couldn't deny his sweet face. And I had a package that belonged to her. "Hopefully she's home."

It was a short walk, only about three strides across the hall to reach the front door to Juliette's condo. My finger found the button to ring her doorbell and I told Thor to sit as I pressed it and waited. He obeyed, sitting quietly beside me as the seconds felt like they stretched into hours. The lock clicked and the door slowly opened.

Juliette was wearing a cotton tank top and shorts. Her hair was pulled up in a messy bun on top of her head. Her eyes widened as they met mine. "Mac? What are you doing here?"

"I'm just getting ready to take Thor for a run, but I have something that belongs to you."

She tilted her head to the side ever so slightly and crossed her arms over her chest as her guard slipped into place. She silently stared at me as I held out the package for her. Her eyes narrowed as she took it from my hands and read the packing label.

"It ended up in my mailbox accidentally."

Juliette tucked the package under her arm as she

lifted her narrowed eyes to mine. "You've had it for a few days."

There was no question, it was a statement.

"I don't check my mail every day, so I didn't get it when it was delivered."

She pursed her lips and her expression was hard to read. If I had to guess, she looked reluctant to believe me, but she didn't press on the issue any further.

"Thank you," she said softly with a nod. Her eyes dropped down to Thor and it was the first time she actually smiled since she opened the door. "I didn't mean to ignore you, buddy." She bent down to scratch behind his ears. "Your owner is a tad annoying, isn't he?"

A chuckle escaped me. "I love when you talk shit about me to my dog."

"It's not talking shit if it's the truth."

Cocking my head to the side, my gaze slowly traveled from her right eye to the left before settling on her right eye again. The ring around her iris was almost black and there were flecks of charcoal in the gray depths. Her right was slightly darker than her left. "One day you're going to feel differently about me."

Juliette's eyes widened and her spine straightened but she quickly snorted to cover up her shock. "That's doubtful," she scoffed and took a step back with her hand on the door. "Thanks for delivering the package that belonged to me."

"I could have kept it," I said with a shrug as the corners of my lips twitched. "But you're welcome."

She glared at me as she slowly began to shut the door. "Go put on a damn shirt before someone gets into a car accident staring at you."

Her voice was barely audible, as if she only meant for herself to hear the words she mumbled, but I heard them. I stared at her door as she closed it and put a barrier between us. My lips broke out into a grin and I shook my head as I ran a hand through my hair.

She was going to drive me fucking insane.

And I was going to love every second of it.

———

Thor kept up the pace with me as we went for a run around the city. The route that I had mapped out that we ran ended up being a little over five miles. It helped with Thor's energy and by the time we reached the condo building, he was walking at a much slower pace. I stopped by the front door and bent down to give him a drink of water before we headed back inside.

The cool air from the air conditioning slid across my skin that was slick with sweat. The Florida heat and humidity was no joke. Usually I tried to get out earlier in the day or late in the evening, not in the middle of the morning like today. It was definitely hotter than I liked it to be while we went for a run, but we survived and got through it.

It just meant that practice this afternoon was going to be a lot harder on my tired muscles.

The elevator ride to my floor was quick and Thor walked beside me as we stepped into the hall. It was quiet, but the sound of his panting was loud as hell, echoing around us as we moved to my door. My key slid into the lock and I turned it over before reaching for the handle.

"You defiled my book."

I slowly turned back around from my door and met Juliette's gaze from across the hall. Her slender legs moved and she stepped closer to me with her arms crossed defensively over her chest.

"Excuse me?" I asked her with my eyebrows pinched together.

She huffed and the irritation was written across her facial expression. "I didn't order a used book and there is stuff written throughout it."

"And you think it was me?"

Juliette uncrossed her arms and planted her hands on her hips with the book in one hand as she stared me down. There was something about the way she was staring at me that demanded my full attention. I couldn't look away from her—I didn't want to. The anger was rolling off her in waves, rippling against my own skin.

Fuck, she was hot like this.

"Mac."

I shook my head, shaking away thoughts of having her underneath me. "What?"

"I know it was you who did it."

"Okay… well, did you even bother reading any of it?"

She curled her top lip in distaste. "No. I merely flipped through the pages and found shit written throughout the margins."

A smile lifted my own lips. "Just read it and then decide if you're really pissed off at me or not."

"I didn't buy the book to have it ruined."

I tilted my head to the side, racking my brain for what the book looked like. I didn't remember it being anything but a normal paperback book, but now I was second-guessing the little notes I left for her to find. "Was it a special edition or something?"

"Well, no," she said, shifting her weight on her feet. "But that is beside the point. It wasn't yours to do that to."

"Are you an only child?"

Juliette gave me a confused look. "What?"

"You are, aren't you?" I snickered. The reaction I was getting from her was priceless. I knew I should have walked away and stopped pissing her off, but she was making this too easy. It was too much fun right now.

"Actually no, I'm not. But what does that have to do with you writing in my book?"

I laughed and shook my head at her. "You clearly

don't know how to share." I exhaled slowly and took a step closer to her as I took the book from her hand. I flipped through the pages until I landed on one that I left a note on. Leaving the book open, I turned it toward her and pressed it against her chest.

Her movements were slow, her eyes never leaving mine as she lifted her hands to take the book from me. Lifting one hand, I brushed a stray lock of hair away from her face, pushing it behind her ear, my fingers lingering on her skin.

"Just read it, Juliette. Read the book and the notes inside, and then you can scream at me."

Her throat bobbed as she swallowed roughly. I took a step away from her, moving until I was back at my door. Juliette's gaze broke away from mine and she looked down at the page I had left open for her. Her eyes widened as they scanned the page and a pink tint blossomed across her cheeks.

Her eyes flashed to mine. The corners of my mouth twitched.

"Or maybe you'll scream for me instead…"

Her lips parted and a ragged breath escaped her. My cock was already hard and I did nothing to hide it. Instead, I spun on my heel and left her in the hallway, still clutching her book as I locked myself and Thor back in my condo.

It was a dirty play, but I never claimed to play fairly.

I was truly looking forward to the consequences now.

CHAPTER EIGHT
JULIETTE

My eyes scanned the page once more, reading Mac's sloppy handwriting that was scratched alongside of the printed text.

Tell me, Juliette. Is this what you like? Is this what you want?

My stomach dipped. I lifted my head off the couch, glancing around my living room like someone may have caught me blushing. After Mac left me pissed off in the hallway, I marched back inside and flopped down on the couch and began reading. I hadn't moved in at least three hours and I was sucked into the story, along with reading the little things he marked and wrote down.

He was smooth, I'd give him that. I had an idea of what his motive was behind this and unfortunately for me, it was working.

Mac Sullivan had my attention, even if I didn't want him to. I couldn't erase this moment from my mind. I couldn't erase the words he wrote inside the book. They were branded in my memory. I wanted to hear the words slip from his lips. I wanted to feel them whispered against the shell of my ear.

I would never admit it out loud to him, but it was a thought I could keep to myself. He was an idiot, if we were being real here. He knew exactly who I was and what that could mean for his career if he decided to be involved with me. For whatever reason, he lacked common sense. Either he didn't care or he really didn't understand. My father would make sure Mac Sullivan was on the first plane out of Orchid City if he decided to pursue me.

And for some reason, that made the temptation even stronger.

Knowing it was something neither of us should be doing made it that much more enticing. I was bored and Mac was just the thing to occupy my time.

I didn't want him to ruin his career, so perhaps there was a way we could make it work without getting caught. Then again, the thought of him leaving Orchid City was also appealing. If he were gone, I wouldn't have to worry about him. I could continue on with my life the way it was before he infiltrated my every thought.

Closing the book, I set it down on the coffee table and finally rose from the couch. There was no sense in locking myself away in my apartment. I needed to confront him head-on.

I walked across the hall, leaving my own door hanging open as I reached his. It was going to be a quick conversation and I wasn't sure what the hell I was even going to say to him. As my fist connected with his door, regret flooded me. This was a terrible mistake. Just because he was being flirty and forward didn't mean I needed to reciprocate that energy. I needed to turn around and walk back into my own condo and pretend he didn't even exist.

Thor started barking on the other side of the door and I shifted my weight nervously on my feet as I waited. Anxiety raced through my body. There was nothing I could do now. I made my decision, so I had to go with it.

A few minutes felt like an eternity, but Mac never came to the door. Judging by the way Thor was barking and whining, it was safe to say Mac wasn't home. A sigh of relief passed through my lips and my heart rate dropped back to a normal rhythm in my chest. I looked back and forth, unsure of what to do now. He would surely be home later, so I could always try again then. I didn't have his phone number, so this was the only way I could actually speak with him.

Turning on my heel, I walked across the hall and back into my apartment. I found a stack of sticky notes inside one of the drawers in my kitchen and I grabbed a pen. The ink marring the paper as I wrote my phone number and nothing else. Mac Sullivan may have appeared to be an idiot, but I had an inkling that he actually wasn't.

He would either use my number or he wouldn't. It was up to him now, and I was perfectly fine with that. I may have wanted him, but I didn't need him. If I didn't hear from him, that was the verification I needed that he was simply fucking with me. All of his flirty actions were about to be challenged. I walked back across the hall and left the note on his door before going back home.

If he wanted to play, I would show him what it looked like to lose.

My stomach growled and I looked down at it in betrayal as I slowly climbed out of the bath. There was a part of me that hated my days off. I needed something to occupy my time or else I would end up leaving notes on my hot neighbor's door.

I sighed to myself. Boredom was never a good thing for me.

My legs were itching to burn from skating, but the kids didn't have practice until tomorrow evening. There was an open hockey session earlier in the day, but I ended up reading through the time. Now, there was just a public skate later tonight that I could go to. It wasn't really ideal because skating in circles could be boring, but I just needed something to block out the noise of the world around me.

And something to distract my mind from my damn neighbor.

I dressed in warm clothing for skating and headed into my kitchen. The cupboards and fridge were practically bare, considering I was inept when it came to cooking. I never swore that I had any qualities that implied I would be a homemaker in my lifetime. After realizing I had nothing easy to make, I grabbed my purse and keys and headed out into the hall. Just as I was locking my door, I saw Mac standing by his, holding the Post-it note that I left.

He lifted his head, his eyes meeting mine as a slow smile formed on his lips. "We really need to stop meeting like this. It's always in the middle of the hall in passing."

I couldn't help myself as I smiled back at him. "It's quite unfortunate, isn't it?"

Mac looked at the note and back at me, chewing on the inside of his cheek. "Wherever you're going, do you have to be there at a certain time?"

I shook my head, not following where he was going with this.

"Good," he said, sliding his key into the lock. "Go back inside."

My forehead creased. "Why? I need to go get food, Mac. I'm starving."

His nostrils flared and his jaw ticked. "Just go back inside, Juliette. You will see."

I narrowed my eyes, irritation sliding through my veins as I huffed and spun around before walking back into my condo. Shutting the door behind me, I stood just on the other side of it. Mac Sullivan was fucking annoying, but I was curious to see what he was actually planning here.

My phone vibrated in the pocket of my pants and I pulled it out, seeing a message from an unfamiliar number on the screen.

UNKNOWN
> Thank you for actually listening to me.

I stared at my phone for a moment, unable to fight the grin that pulled on my lips. I knew it was Mac before I even opened the message. Who else would it be, considering he had just found the note that I left with my number for him?

JULIETTE
> I never once claimed to be a compliant person.

MAC
> No, you didn't. And you are most certainly the most difficult person I've ever met.

JULIETTE
> Why did you send me back into my condo?

MAC

Because I wanted to get to use your phone number and pretend that I got to text you before running into you again.

The stupid smile on my face wouldn't go away and I shook my head to myself as I typed out another response to him. We were standing across the hall from one another with only our doors separating us as we texted back and forth.

JULIETTE

Can I come out yet?

MAC

Nope. I'm not done yet.

What are you doing this evening?

JULIETTE

I was going to go get something to eat and then go to Orchid City Ice Rink for the public skate later.

MAC

Yuck. You want to go skate in circles with a bunch of people who are holding on to the boards or look like a newborn giraffe on skates?

JULIETTE

Don't sound like such a pompous asshole. Not all of us have access to a private practice facility. And if you don't remember, there was a time in your life when you looked like one of those newborn giraffes, so be kind.

MAC

Let me come with you.

My eyes widened as I stared down at my phone, reading his message three times. It was the last response I expected from him.

MAC

I know you're there, Juliette. Don't go silent on me now.

JULIETTE

Why would you want to come along? You don't want to go skate in circles with the public.

MAC

You're right. It sounds fucking boring, but if you're going I want to go too.

Plus, I haven't eaten yet either.

I couldn't help the nervousness that raced through me.

JULIETTE

Didn't you just get home from practice? You're probably exhausted.

MAC

If you don't want me to come along, you can just say that.

There was a part of me that didn't want him to. The cautious part of my brain told me I needed to stay away. I needed to burn the book he wrote little notes for me in and forget he even existed. He could be my neighbor who played for the team my father coached and that would be it. We didn't have to be friends. We didn't have to do things together.

The impulsive part of my brain won the battle tonight.

JULIETTE

Don't bother me when we're on the ice.

MAC

Deal.

CHAPTER NINE
MAC

Juliette sat quietly in the passenger seat as she stared out the window. I was surprised when she agreed to let me come with her. When I asked her where she was planning on eating, she proved that she wasn't as planned and calculated as she appeared. Her response was that she was going to go downtown and walk down the street until she found the place that seemed most appealing.

It wasn't something I would normally do, but I was along for the ride and just following Juliette's lead.

Cars lined the street as we pulled into the main downtown area. It was a little shopping district that was lined with stores and restaurants. It was almost always busy, especially this time of year when there were a lot of tourists that came down south for the warmer weather. I was able to find an empty parking spot and pulled my car into it before putting it in park and killing the engine.

Juliette was already climbing out before I had the chance to open the door for her. I didn't want to scare her off by making it seem like a date, so I ignored the nagging inside me that said I needed to treat her that way.

"Where to?" I asked her as we stood side by side on the bustling sidewalk.

Juliette looked up and down the street, her eyes narrowing as she scanned all the various signs. She turned her head to the left and stared for a moment before nodding in that direction. "Let's go this way."

I fell into step beside her as we walked past a few groups of people waiting outside of some of the restaurants. It was a busy night, so we would most likely have a wait anywhere we went.

"Is this what you usually do? You just roll the dice and end up wherever it may be?"

Juliette glanced at me, her charcoal eyes meeting mine. From the corner of my eye, I saw someone heading in her direction, not paying attention to where they were going. Grabbing for her, I pulled Juliette from their path. She gasped and stumbled into me. The floral scent of her perfume infiltrated my nose and I couldn't help myself as my grip tightened on her arms.

She stared up at me, her lips parting slightly as if we were frozen in time. I couldn't help myself as my gaze traveled down to her mouth. She was standing so close, her chest nearly brushing against me. My heart pounded inside my chest, my fingers on the soft skin of her arms. My eyes drifted back to hers.

Snapping out of my stupor, I released her, taking a step back as I cleared my throat. "Sorry. That guy wasn't paying attention and he was about to run into you."

Her eyes bounced back and forth between mine before she straightened her spine and squared her jaw. "Thanks."

I nodded awkwardly and Juliette turned away from me, leading the way again. I followed along with her, our arms brushing against one another's as we walked. It was hard to ignore the electricity that sizzled along my nerve endings every time she touched me, but I did. I didn't move away, though. I craved the way she felt, the way she smelled.

"To answer your question, yes. I don't do this with most aspects of my life, but I'm not good at deciding where to eat." She paused and glanced at me from the corner of her eye with a ghost of a smile. "It's easier if I just let my stomach lead the way."

"I like that," I agreed, smiling back at her.

I like you.

Juliette abruptly stopped in front of a small cafe. *Ain't That a Bisque*. She turned to look at me. "Let's eat here."

I looked at the cafe, noticing there was one empty table and not a line. There wouldn't be an issue with us eating here and we wouldn't have to wait an obscene amount of time just to get seated. My eyes met hers. "Perfect."

We ordered our food at the counter and found the empty table while we waited. The menu mainly consisted of soups, salads, and sandwiches. I wasn't going to complain because everything looked and smelled delicious.

Juliette took the seat across from me and folded her arms on the table. "I'm still mad at you for what you did to my book."

My mouth twitched. "Are you really, though?"

She leveled her gaze with mine, staring at me with a blank look on her face for a moment. Her expression cracked, a blush crept across her face, and she smiled as she ducked her head. She toyed with her glass of water on the table before looking up at me through her thick lashes.

"No, I'm not."

"So, that means you read it then?" I questioned her, my voice hoarse and low.

Juliette lifted her head. "Some of it."

"Hmm," I murmured as I took a sip of my own drink while I continued to study her. "No comment on any of it?"

"I'm still processing," she countered as she glanced past me before her gaze met mine again. "I'll let you know when I'm ready to talk about it."

"Take your time," I told her as the buzzer went off,

signaling that our food was ready to be collected. I slowly rose to my feet, picking up the device as my eyes never left hers. I didn't expect her to bring up the notes now, but eventually we would be talking about them.

Or exploring the subject further.

"I'm not going anywhere."

Juliette was more forthcoming than I imagined she would be. She kept her cards close to her chest, but she wasn't withholding information like I expected. Most of the questions I asked her were bullshit ones. I discovered her favorite color was pink—surprisingly—her favorite food was soup, and she loved fall weather when the leaves were changing colors.

She was telling me all about the team of six-year-olds she was coaching as we approached the rink. I loved the way her face lit up as she told me about the kids and their quirks. The ones who could skate better than the others. And the little girl, Sydney, that she had high hopes for.

As I pulled into the parking lot, I couldn't help myself as I looked over at Juliette. Her cheeks were flushed and her eyes were bright and filled with joy.

"Why don't you play anymore?"

Just like that, the fire in her eyes had been extinguished. Pain washed over her irises and the smile fell from her face. "It wasn't by choice," she said quietly. I moved my car into an empty parking spot and turned off the engine. "A stupid mistake took everything away from me."

I turned to look at her, meeting her pained look. "We don't have to talk about it if you don't want to."

She shook her head dismissively and shrugged. "It doesn't matter anymore. In college I was at a party with a friend and I didn't realize how drunk she was when we went to leave. She got behind the wheel and hit a tree on our way home. The impact was on my side. I shattered my left femur and my right ankle and hip. I was a fucking mess from the waist down. It took a long time to recover and a lot of time off the ice. I can never play like I used to."

Guilt consumed me—guilt for asking so she would open up to me, and weirdly guilt for being able to play professionally when she physically couldn't. I couldn't imagine being in that position, of losing everything you had worked so hard for.

"I'm sorry, Juliette," I said softly as my hand instinctively reached out for hers. She didn't deny me as I slid my palm against hers and gave her fingers a squeeze. "I can't imagine and I'm so sorry that happened to you."

A nervous laugh slipped from her lips and she pulled her hand from mine. "It's fine, Mac. I don't need your pity. Life doesn't always work out the way we think it will."

Silence encapsulated us and her pain was palpable. I studied her for a moment as she shifted uncomfortably in her seat. She leaned forward, grabbing her backpack that had her skates inside before she reached for the door handle. She climbed out without another word, softly shutting the door behind her.

My chest heaved as I breathed deeply, almost regretting bringing up the subject. I got out of the car and walked to the trunk to fetch my skates. Juliette waited along the side of the car, typing something out on her phone. When I approached her, she looked up at me and slid her phone back into her pocket.

"Remember what I said before we left," she warned me as we began to walk toward the building. "As soon as we're on the ice, I don't want to be bothered."

"Noted," I said with a nod of understanding. "When you step out on the ice, everything gets quiet, doesn't it?"

Juliette whipped her head to look at me as I held the door open for her. She nodded, tilting her head to the side.

"It's the same for me too."

She looked as if she were going to say something but decided against it. Juliette walked past me, marching up to the front desk as I followed behind her. She insisted on paying for both of us and I let her because I was learning not to argue with her unless I truly wanted a fight. We walked out to the rink and there were people all over the place lacing their skates.

"It's busy," I noted as we found an empty spot on the bench.

Juliette pulled out her skates and began to tie them. "It will be fine. Just stay on the inside since a lot of people will be along the boards."

"I'll follow your lead."

Her eyes sliced to mine. "No, you won't."

I stifled a laugh and shook my head. "No, I won't."

Juliette rose to her feet and even though she told me not to, I fell into step after her as she walked over to the door. She reached into her pocket, pulling out her earbuds, and put them in. The blades of her skates hit the ice and she skated away, leaving me where I was standing.

I headed out onto the ice and chased after her. Juliette moved like a skilled skater, her edges cutting through the surface as she navigated the rink. I was completely captivated by her. Power rippled through my muscles and I pushed off and moved behind her. We circled around the rink three times with some distance between us before I said fuck it.

Juliette was unsuspecting as I crept up behind her. Reaching for her, I plucked one of the earbuds from her ear. Her eyes widened and she spun around to glare at me as she began to skate backward.

"What the hell, Sullivan?!" she yelled at me over the loud voices echoing within the glass perimeter.

A smirk lifted my lips. "If you want it, come get it."

She was still in shock as I quickly ducked past her and took off around the rink. My stride was longer and I stayed ahead of Juliette, but she was applying the pressure. She was on my heels, chasing after me. As I skated past the left corner, I shifted sideways, my skates cutting deeply into the ice as I abruptly stopped.

Juliette didn't anticipate the movement and I didn't realize how close she was. She tried to stop, but was a fraction of a second too late. She crashed into me, showing no mercy as her hands went for mine. Laughter spilled from my lips and I tried to brace the brunt of the collision as we both fell onto the ice. The surface was cold and wet, soaking through my pants as Juliette laid on top of me.

The lilt of her laughter warmed my soul as we fought over the earbud. Her fingers were wrapped around mine and I relaxed as I let her wrench them apart before closing them again. She fought against me and we were both out of breath as she finally pulled my hands open and picked up the earbud that was in my palm.

"You're so goddamn annoying," she huffed, the laughter still in her voice as she pushed away from me and rose to her feet. A smile was on her lips as she held her hand out to me.

I took it and climbed to my feet, our hands still latched together. "Let me skate with you."

She stared at me for a moment, pursing her lips, her chest still heaving with every breath she took. She held her other hand out to me, giving the earbud back to me as a ghost of a smile danced across her mouth. Her eyes shimmered under the lights above. "Fine."

I let go of her hand and accepted the AirPod before putting it in my ear. The sound of the music she was playing beat against my eardrum as my heart pounded in my chest. We fell into stride together as we began to skate around the rink. She didn't leave me behind, opting to stay with me the entire time.

There was already a crack in the walls she had put up around herself.

And I was determined to tear them to the ground.

CHAPTER TEN
JULIETTE

"Juliette. Do you have a few minutes to talk before you leave?"

Dante's voice broke through the silence as I was untying my skates after practice. Lifting my head, I looked up at him and sat upright while cleaning the ice from my blades. Anxiety instantly balled in the pit of my stomach. I nodded, keeping my mouth shut. All of the kids were on their way out of the rink and the next group was getting ready to go on the ice for practice.

"Perfect," he said with a smile and a nod. "Come see me in my office when you're finished."

A week or so had passed since I last spoke with him in regards to me working a paid position for the club. Dante excused himself from the locker room and I finished getting my things together before I headed off to find him in his office. It was a small room with a desk in the center. Trophies were on a shelf behind him, along with framed jerseys and pictures of winning teams from tournaments.

Dante looked up as I knocked on the opened door. He smiled brightly when he saw me and motioned for me to take a seat across from him. "How was practice today?"

"It went really well. It's been so enjoyable coaching these kids and watching them progress." I paused for a moment as I sat down. "They all seem to love it so much."

"We have heard nothing but great things about you, Juliette. We are so glad to have you here with us. The kids are really thriving with your help."

Heat crept across my face and I nervously tucked a hair behind my ear. Compliments weren't something I was good at accepting. They tended to make me feel uncomfortable. "Thank you. Thank you for such an amazing opportunity and for taking a chance on me by letting me help."

"You've become a vital part of the team here. I know we had already spoken a bit already about the paid position, and the club would like to move forward with that." He paused, his eyes searching mine. "If you are still interested, that is."

My heart skipped a beat in my chest as excitement washed over me. I had been working a job I absolutely hated, and this was my chance to leave that all behind to do what I actually loved doing. "I am definitely interested."

"Perfect. The plan is for me to shift into more of a general manager position, where I oversee everything with the rink and essentially the bullshit. We'd have you as the youth development coordinator, so all things with youth hockey would go through you." Dante pulled out a packet of papers and handed them to me. "Also, I think your marketing background could be extremely beneficial to the club."

I nodded, my eyes briefly scanning over the job description and duties. "What about coaching?"

Dante studied me for a moment. "Is that something you're interested in still doing?"

"I would have enough time to, wouldn't I?" I asked him.

"We can certainly make sure you do. We will keep you on as a coach, if you would like that."

"I would." I smiled. "If it is all right, I need to give my two weeks' notice at my current job and then I would be able to start."

"Of course." He returned my smile. "If you want to, take the time tonight to go over everything I've given you and give me a call in the morning with your official answer. Then we can have it slated for you to start in two weeks. That also gives me time to transition everything over to you."

"That is perfect." I rose from my seat, grabbing my bag from the floor beside me as I tucked the stack of papers beneath my arm. "Thank you again, Dante. I will call you in the morning."

Dante held his hand out for me to shake. "No, thank you, Juliette. You don't know how valued you are here."

I couldn't help but laugh. "It's only been a few weeks. Are you sure about that?"

Dante's expression was serious as he nodded again. "Your father put in a good word for you and you have proven yourself."

I stared at him for a moment, a little taken aback from his words. My father and I had a strained relationship since the accident in college. He was extremely pissed because I was foolish. He had such high hopes for my future in hockey and I threw it all away with one drunken mistake. A lot of things were said out of anger and disappointment.

And there was a part of me that never forgave him for it.

He had tried over the years, but things were still tense between us. He never brought up what happened or the things he said. He never even apologized for it. Instead, he simply brushed it all away as if his hurtful words were never said. As if he didn't make me feel like absolute shit for losing the one thing that meant the most to me.

Dante and I finished up our conversation and I excused myself from his office before heading out to my car. After starting the engine, I pulled out my phone and tapped on my father's contact info to call him.

"Juliette, is everything okay? I just got back from Calgary."

It wasn't often that I called him out of nowhere. Usually a text was sent before I would even bother calling and if I needed to talk to my parents, my mother was always the safer choice.

"Yes. I wanted to call you to thank you for putting in a good word for me with Dante. He said you vouched for me and told him everything about my history with hockey."

My father was silent for a beat before he spoke again. "You don't have to thank me, Juliette. It was the least I could do." He paused, and I picked at the skin around my thumbnail. "You'll never be able to play like you did before, but I know how badly you still want a life playing the game. It's just a different way of doing that."

The guilt and regret was heavy in his tone. It wasn't the first time he said something to the same degree and in a way, I knew it was his way of trying to apologize. I would never get a full apology from the man, but it was time for me to let it go and forgive him.

"I really do appreciate it. I just accepted a position as the youth development coordinator there and will still get to coach the little kids."

"That's absolutely amazing." I could hear the smile in his voice as he spoke. "You've always been destined for great things, and I know this will be a great venture for you."

"I should probably go, but I just wanted to say thank you," I told him, suddenly feeling uncomfortable with the conversation. Just like he didn't apologize, I didn't like having moments like this that warmed my heart.

"You're my daughter, Juliette. I know we've had issues in the past, but that is one thing that will never change. I will always do anything I can to help you." He fell silent, and I waited for him to speak again. "If you ever want to come to a Vipers game, let me know. I'll have a seat for you."

"Thanks, Dad, I will."

We both said "I love you" and I quickly ended the call to avoid any more uncomfortable conversation. He may not have apologized, but it was still a step in the direction of forgiveness. Our relationship still had a chance, as long as we both put our stubbornness to the side.

When I got back to my condo building, I grabbed my mail and took the elevator up to my floor. Thankfully, all of my things were in my mailbox this time, but there was a part of me that wished Mac had stolen another package.

It would have given me an excuse to see him again.

An entire week had almost passed since we went skating together. He was busy with hockey and was due to be back from a trip they took for an away game.

My father had answered the phone, saying he just got back from Calgary, so that would mean Mac was back too. Unless he was out or ended up going somewhere else for the night.

I wasn't sure what he really did with his spare time and it wasn't any of my business… even if I wanted to make it my business.

As I walked up to my door, something caught my eye. Butterflies flickered to life in my stomach and I pulled the sticky note from my door. My eyes scanned over the words scratched in his messy handwriting and a smile drifted across my lips.

> *Notes are fun, aren't they?*
> *It's your turn now, Juliette.*
> *Just kidding, I don't want to wait until tomorrow to find a note from you. Text me when you get home.*

A soft laugh left my lips as I shook my head and tucked his note into my pocket. I glanced over my shoulder as I unlocked my door, hoping that maybe he was standing there, but he wasn't. Slipping inside my condo, I pulled my phone out and found the message thread between us. My fingers tapped on the screen while my heart beat erratically in my chest. I hated the effect he had on me while loving it at the same time.

He made me feel such conflicting things, and I knew nothing good would ever come from any of this.

JULIETTE
I got the note you left. Welcome home.

MAC
Come over and welcome me home yourself.

I stared at my phone with my feet cemented to the floor as I read his message a second time. Then a third time. The words didn't change. They stared back at me, taunting me. I knew better than to get involved with someone like him. Mac Sullivan was everything I did and didn't want.

JULIETTE
Give me twenty minutes.

MAC
I'll be waiting for you.

CHAPTER ELEVEN
MAC

Thor grunted as he rolled onto his back on the couch beside me. I looked over at him and scratched his stomach as he pushed his black nose against my thigh. A soft knock sounded from my door and Thor's body wiggled as he rolled onto the floor and galloped across the living room. Excitement rippled through me and my footsteps were light as I followed after him.

I was definitely playing with fire.

I didn't expect Juliette to take the bait. I imagined she would tell me to fuck off when I told her to come over, but she surprised me and agreed.

Consequences be damned—I wanted her and I was done denying myself of the simple pleasures in life.

Her gray eyes met mine as I pulled open the door and found her standing in the hall. She was wearing a pair of black yoga pants, an oversized crewneck hoodie, and her damp hair was pulled back in a braid. Face free of makeup, she was absolutely breathtaking.

"Hey," I said softly, as I pushed Thor back with my leg and held the door open for her. "I wasn't sure you were going to come over."

Torment flickered in her eyes. "I probably shouldn't have."

I tilted my head to the side. "I have no expectations, Juliette. I just wanted to see you."

"Why would you want to see me, Mac?" She closed the distance between us until her toes reached mine. Her braid fell down her back as she lifted her chin to look at me. "Why me?"

Her questions were unexpected. There was conflict woven within her expression and I wasn't sure where it was coming from. She was off-limits to me, so if there was anyone who should feel conflicted here, it shouldn't have been her. I should have closed the door in that moment and erased her from my mind, but I couldn't.

"Because I can't get you out of my head. No matter what I do to try and forget about you, you're still there. My thoughts continuously circle back to you." I swallowed roughly, running a frustrated hand through my hair. An exasperated sigh escaped me as I stared into the burning flames in her irises. "I'm not allowed to have you, and that only makes me want you more."

Juliette lifted up onto the balls of her feet as she slid her hands around the back of my head. There was no hesitation as she pulled my face down to hers, our mouths colliding. Her lips were soft like butter melting against mine. Instinctively, I wrapped my arms around her waist, pulling her body closer. Moving my feet, I spun her around and began to walk her into my place while I kicked the door shut behind us.

"We shouldn't be doing this," she whispered against my lips.

"Shh." I nipped at her bottom lip. "You're not the one who could lose everything."

"That's exactly why we should stop."

Juliette didn't move away from me as I pushed her up against the wall in the living room. My hands scaled her body until my fingers were fisted in her hair. Her lips parted as my tongue slid along the seam of her mouth. She opened for me, her tongue like silk against mine. She tasted faintly of mint and I swallowed the moan that she let out as I ground my pelvis against her.

"If you want me to stop, all you have to do is say the words, babe. If not, I have no plan on stopping and I couldn't care less about the fucking consequences of having you."

She didn't push me away. Instead, she slid her hands along my scalp, gripping the tousled waves as she held my face above hers.

"Don't."

My mouth twitched and I lightly pressed my lips to hers. "Don't what?"

Tension hung heavily in the air between us. Her

chest rose and fell with every shallow breath she took. I loved seeing her like this—like a fucking mess. A mess that I created.

"Don't stop."

No other words needed to be spoken. My mouth captured hers and it was suddenly a race to the bedroom, except we never even made it that far. She lifted her arms as I grabbed the hem of her sweatshirt and began to haul it up her torso. We only broke apart for me to lift it over her head before doing the same with my own. I pulled her away from the wall and began backing her into the kitchen, my leg between hers, guiding her as I reached around her back to undo the strap of her bra.

Juliette stopped as she reached the island in the kitchen. I dropped her bra onto the floor and slid my hands down under her ass, lifting her into the air and setting her down on the counter. My hands drifted along the waistband of her pants just as she slipped her fingers beneath mine. I couldn't fight back the moan as our tongues danced with one another's.

My hands dropped down to my waist and I shoved my pants and boxer briefs down my thighs. Juliette was lifting up her ass and taking her pants off as I reached for her so I could finish the job. Taking a step away from her, I stripped her until she was completely bare.

"Your pussy is glistening," I murmured as I tentatively ran a finger along her center. She moaned, writhing beneath my touch. "You're so ready for me, aren't you?"

"Mac," she sighed as she leaned back and propped herself on her elbows.

"Tell me what you want, Juliette."

She stifled another moan as I slipped a finger inside her and slowly began to push it in and out.

"You," she said breathlessly. "I want you."

"Fuck," I breathed raggedly as I stared at her spread out on my kitchen counter. My arms slipped under the backs of her knees and I hauled her to the edge of the counter as I lowered myself to the floor. "I've spent many nights dreaming of what you taste like. I can't wait to finally find out."

My face dipped down between her legs, but she roughly grabbed my hair, almost as if she were going to pull my head away. She surprised me as she guided me and I smiled just before running my tongue against her. A low groan rumbled in my throat. My cock throbbed. She tasted like fucking heaven and I was going to devour her.

Juliette mumbled something unintelligible as I continued to lick her pussy, circling my tongue around her clit. My movements were deliberately slow and teasing as I fucked her with my mouth. My tongue slid along her center before flattening over her clit over and over. Her hands abandoned my hair and I looked up at her as she lay back on the counter.

I wanted this memory—this moment—cemented in my mind for the rest of eternity.

My hands slid down to grip her ass as I held her firmly in place. My fingertips dug into her flesh and I swirled my tongue around her clit again, feeling her slowly coming undone at the seams. Moans spilled from her lips as she murmured my name.

The sounds she made was all I needed to keep going. She shifted her hips, lifting them to meet me as I continued to work my tongue against her. A smirk pulled on my lips and I looked up from my position on my knees to watch as much of her body as I could as I tasted her. She was holding on, for whatever reason, almost as if she didn't want to experience the euphoria when she finally fell over the edge.

Her legs began to shake, her hips bucking as she lifted her head from the counter and intertwined her fingers in my hair again. "Oh god, Mac," she half moaned, half cried out. "I'm so close."

"Come for me, Juliette. I want to taste your pleasure on my tongue."

She raised her voice, my name a cry as her orgasm tore through her body. Her legs instinctively went to move together and I pinned them down, not moving away as I continued to ravage her. I was addicted to her taste, addicted to her touch.

I was irrevocably fucked.

My movements were slow as I lazily lapped at her, licking and tasting every last drop until she was fully satiated and her orgasm had begun to lull her into a state of euphoric bliss. I pulled away, standing back upright as I looked at her lying on the counter. She lifted her head and her lips parted with a ragged breath as her gaze clashed with mine. There was a pinkish tint spread across her cheeks and her chest rose and fell in rapid succession.

She was absolutely fucking perfect.

I could get used to this.

Raking my hands over her body, I stepped closer and positioned myself between her legs but made no move to slip inside her. Her skin was soft like silk beneath my palms and my fingertips continued to roam over the smooth planes of her flesh.

"What the hell was that?" She laughed breathlessly as she gave me a shy, innocent smile.

"That, my love," I started, as I grabbed my cock and slid it through her juices before pressing it against her center. She wiggled beneath me, desperate to feel me inside, so I gave her what she wanted. She collapsed back onto the counter, moaning loudly as I thrust into her. "Was just the beginning."

CHAPTER TWELVE
JULIETTE

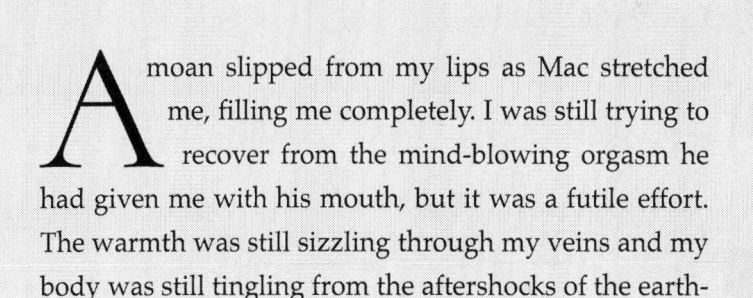

A moan slipped from my lips as Mac stretched me, filling me completely. I was still trying to recover from the mind-blowing orgasm he had given me with his mouth, but it was a futile effort. The warmth was still sizzling through my veins and my body was still tingling from the aftershocks of the earthquake I experienced.

There wasn't a part of me that thought Mac wouldn't be good at any of this, but the way he worked his tongue against me. Jesus Christ. It was like there were fireworks exploding behind my eyelids as my orgasm hit me like a tidal wave. No one had ever made me come like that before. No one had ever made me feel that fucking good.

And as he slowly stroked my insides, gently pistoning his hips, I realized I had underestimated him completely. The guys I had been with before were always more concerned with their own pleasure. I was beginning to realize that wasn't the case with Mac. If it were, he wouldn't have dropped to his knees to feast between my legs before sliding inside me.

Instinctively, I wrapped my legs around Mac's waist, holding on to him as he began to pick up the pace. His hands slid to my thighs and he pulled them open, clicking his tongue at me as I lifted my head to look up at him.

"You're blocking me, sunshine."

My brows furrowed, but the expression on my face only lasted a fraction of a second as he thrust in deeper than before, causing my eyes to practically roll back in my head. "What do you mean?" I half panted as I straightened my chin to look at him.

"You feel how deep I am inside you right now?" His voice was hoarse and thick with lust. "I can't get in there like this when your legs are around me. I like you spread open and ready with your pussy glistening under the light." His fingertips dug into my flesh as he tightened his grip on me. "I have you exactly where I want you right now."

"Are you the one who is in charge right now?"

The corners of his mouth twitched and he thrust harder. "I'm always in charge, Juliette. If you want to pretend to be in control, I'll entertain the thought."

Mac reached between us, pressing his palm against my pelvis as his skilled thumb found my clit. He applied pressure to the bundle of nerves and lazily began to move his thumb in a circular motion while he continued to slide in and out of me. My body twitched and the fire was lit inside my stomach once again.

"I want to watch you come," he murmured as he slid his other hand down to cup my ass. "I want to see how you look while you come all over my cock."

With the way he was moving his hand, along with his dick inside of me, it wasn't going to take long for that to happen. I was still riding out the waves from my previous orgasm and could feel another coming on again.

"Are you going to come too?" I moaned, fighting the urge to collapse back onto the counter again.

"I'm not worried about me right now," he murmured, applying more pressure to my clit as he began to work his thumb faster. "I want to take care of you, over and over… and then I'll get mine."

Holy fucking shit.

Hearing those words from him had my body about to transport into another dimension.

Mac's eyes never left mine. His hips never changed pace. They moved in long, slow strokes as he slid in deep and slowly pulled halfway out before repeating the same torturous movements. His thumb was driving me absolutely insane. Warmth continued to build within the pit of my stomach, rapidly spilling into my veins as I crested the edge of ecstasy.

"Goddamn, look at you right now." Mac watched me with a hooded gaze, his tongue darting out to wet his lips. "Come for me, baby. Let me feel you. Let me hear you."

"Oh god, Mac," I cried out, unable to help myself. I was so close and the longer I held on, the more intense the buildup was.

He didn't stop moving inside me. He didn't stop circling his thumb. Mac Sullivan was relentless and I was coming apart at the seams. I couldn't hold back any longer and my orgasm tore through my body like a fucking force I didn't stand a chance against. I cried out, his name falling from my lips once again as the volcano inside me erupted.

My head fell back against the counter and stars filled my vision as the fire spread through my flesh. My legs were shaking, my entire body betraying me as I came undone. I barely registered Mac's hand leaving my ass until he was leaning over me with his fingers diving into my long locks as he gripped the base of my skull.

He lifted my head from the counter. "Open your eyes, sunshine. Look at me while you lose yourself around my cock."

My eyelids were heavy as if there were bags of sand weighing them down. I peeled them open, meeting his gaze. His nose was almost touching mine and his eyes burned holes through my own as he stared at me with such an intensity that struck me to my core.

"That's it, Juliette," he murmured as his lips nipped at my flesh. "You're so fucking good."

I was a mess beneath him, floating on a euphoric

cloud I never wanted to get off of. Mac stood upright, his hands gripping my hips as he began to move inside me once again. He started to thrust harder, as if he was now lost in his own moment. The pleasure was borderline unbearable and my nails dug into his skin as I held on for dear life.

His hips began to slow and I lifted my head to look up at him in confusion. He threw me off guard, the way he shifted gears by fucking me hard to slowing almost to a stop. He stared down at me and I instantly felt his absence as he pulled out.

Mac's hands slid down to my hips and he pulled me off the counter until I was standing on unsteady feet. My eyes searched his and I couldn't help but instantly feel like I did something wrong. Like he was suddenly rejecting me.

"What are you doing, Mac?"

His fingertips dug into my hips as he abruptly spun me around to face away from him. "I want to fuck you from behind. Are you good with that, sunshine?"

I looked at him over my shoulder as he inched me closer to the counter. The quartz countertop was cold against my stomach and I nodded. He grabbed my chin, his lips colliding with mine as he kissed me deeply.

"You listen so fucking well, I love it."

He released my face as he trailed his lips along my chin and down my throat before pressing them against the nape of my neck. His hand slid along my spine, slowly pressing me forward until my body was flush against the counter.

I pressed my ass back against him and he groaned as his hands found my cheeks. He pushed his knee between my thighs, spreading them open as he slammed inside me without warning. I cried out in surprise and pleasure as he filled me completely with one swift thrust.

"I don't want to hurt you, but I want to fuck you so goddamn hard right now."

Lifting my head from the counter, I looked back at him from the corner of my eye. "Do it, Mac. Fuck me harder."

The fire in his irises burned deeper and darker as he tightened his grip on my ass. Slowly inching out, he paused with just the tip inside of me until he slammed back into me once again. Except this time, he didn't stop. He didn't tease me and torture me like he had been doing the whole time.

He was pounding into me, his balls slapping against me as he fucked me harder with every thrust. I was already seeing stars with the small flecks swirling around in my vision. I couldn't think straight, couldn't see straight. He was fucking me senseless and I never wanted him to stop.

The back-to-back orgasms still had my body tingling and I could already feel myself climbing closer to the edge as he stroked my insides. Releasing one of my ass cheeks, he slid his hand up my spine until he was wrapping his hand around my throat. His body was warm as he leaned forward until his lips grazed the shell of my ear.

"Take it, Juliette," he commanded, nipping at my earlobe. "Take my cock like it belongs this deep inside you."

His words in my ear, his hand on my throat, his cock so deep inside me I could practically feel him in my rib cage. He pounded into me with such force, it was beginning to feel like he was going to split me in two. He could have shattered me into a million pieces and I wouldn't have cared.

My pussy clenched and he groaned as I tightened around the length of his dick. I was breathless, struggling to suck in any oxygen. His grip around my throat was firm and the sounds of him in my ear sent me falling into the abyss. Everything around us ceased to exist as the earth-shattering orgasm completely pulled me under.

Mac straightened his spine, moving away from me as he pounded into me once more before pulling out. The warmth of his cum coated my ass as he lost himself all over me.

"Fuck," he sighed, letting out a shaky breath as we both attempted to recover. "I could stare at you like this for the rest of my life… bent over with your ass up, covered in my cum."

My body was moving on autopilot as my mind wasn't even present anymore. I pushed away from the counter and my legs felt like Jell-O. Mac moved over to the sink and ran a washcloth under the water before walking over to clean me up.

"You don't have to do that," I mumbled, half feeling embarrassed as I realized what the hell just happened between us. I didn't regret it at all, I was just a little shocked because I usually didn't act impulsively like that.

"I know I don't, but I want to."

We both fell silent as he wiped the cum from me and dried my skin before handing me my clothing. Mac had no shame as he stood there completely naked while he watched me get dressed.

"I should probably head home... it's getting pretty late and I have to be up early for work."

Mac studied me, his expression unreadable. His gaze lingered for a moment before he began to get dressed. "I'll walk you to your door."

I didn't argue with him as he placed his hand on the small of my back and guided me back to my condo. I was too out of it to tell if things felt awkward or what. What I needed was to pass out in my bed after three consecutive orgasms like that.

"Thank you for that, Mac," I said quietly as he stood in the hall while I let myself into my place. I turned back to look at him. "That was a little unexpected, but it was good... really good."

A smile pulled on his lips. "You know where to find me if you ever want to do that again."

My lips parted and a shaky breath escaped me.

"Get some sleep, sunshine," he said as he stepped closer to me and pressed his lips to my forehead.

I watched him as he turned around and headed back to his door that was still wide open. "Good night, Mac," I called out to him.

He paused in his doorway, turning back to look at me again. "Sweet dreams, Juliette," he said with a wink. "I hope you see me in them."

Words failed me, yet again, as we both closed our doors at the same time. He continued to leave me speechless, without a single coherent thought.

What the hell was he doing to me?

And why did I like it?

CHAPTER THIRTEEN
MAC

Following Lincoln, Nico, and Wes down the tunnel, we all funneled onto the bench. We had already gone through our normal game day routines—morning practice, pre-game naps, and warm-ups—and now we were ready to start the game. Nico, Wes, Lincoln, Theo, and I headed out onto the ice for the national anthem before we had to take our places around the face-off circle.

The player from the other team gave me a dirty look as we got into position. Nico was in the center of the circle, his knees bent and his stick on the ice, ready to battle for the puck. The ref said something to the two of them, but over the music playing throughout the stadium, I didn't hear what he said.

And it didn't really matter.

No one liked the refs. Half the time they made bullshit calls, or else they didn't call the penalties that needed to be called. They played dirtier than some of the players, it felt like.

The puck hit the ice and Nico won the face-off. He hit the puck with the backhand of his stick, sending it across the ice to Wes. He skated around one of the wingers on the other team and in the direction of their goal. We all made our way down toward the net with Lincoln and I hanging back, since we were the two defensemen.

Wes passed to Theo who made a shot, but the other team stole the puck. My mind wasn't as dialed in as I would have preferred it to be. The other player came skating toward me and I tried to take possession of the puck and he quickly passed to another player before I could deflect it.

It was a move I should have anticipated, but I didn't.

Our shift ended after only twenty seconds and one by one, we made our way back to the bench for a line change. I sat down next to Lincoln and Wes, my body tense, waiting for Coach Anderson to say something about my minor fuckup.

"Get your head out of your ass, Sullivan," he barked from where he was standing behind the bench. "I have no problem benching your ass for the rest of the game if you keep pulling shit like that. You shouldn't have missed that pass."

"Yes, sir."

Wes glanced at me from the corner of his eye. "You do not want to be on his shit list."

"Yeah," Lincoln agreed as we all watched the game continuing on the ice in front of us. "Remember when he benched me in the other game?"

Coach Anderson couldn't hear us, but I didn't want to chime in to their conversation. He had no idea that I fucked his daughter last night and I didn't need to have any other reasons to be on his bad side. There was no way he would find out about the two of us, so I was safe in that aspect. When it came to ice time, I wasn't going to lose any of that.

"Noted," I said to my two friends, keeping my voice down. "I have no desire to make my way onto his bad side."

He was right—I did need to get my head out of my ass.

I needed to stop thinking about his daughter and how good she felt coming on my cock.

We ended up winning the game, thankfully. Coach Anderson was clearly pissed at me for the remainder of the game, but I ended up getting my shit together and played my position the way I needed to. I made sure to not make the same mistake I did during the first period.

After everyone was dressed and ready to leave, I found Lincoln waiting for me by the door. I slowly walked up to him with Wes beside me. Nico was the first to leave, undoubtedly rushing home to Harper. The obsession that man had with her was borderline nauseating.

"I know you probably need to get home to Charlotte, but did you guys want to go get a drink or anything?" Lincoln asked us.

Wes nodded. "Charlotte is in full deadline mode, so I'd rather not go home right now."

I tilted my head to the side. "What does that even mean?" We all knew Wes's girlfriend was an author, but that was the extent of it.

"When it's crunch time for her, it's best to not bother her." Wes let out a soft laugh, shaking his head as the three of us headed out into the parking lot. "She's basically like a cat. I make sure she has food and water and I wait for her to come to me for attention. Other than that, I keep my distance and try my best not to bother her."

A light bulb went off in my brain as my mind drifted to the book Juliette had ordered. "Charlotte writes romance, right?"

Wes's eyebrows scrunched together and he nodded. "Yeah, why? You don't read, Sullivan."

"Yeah, no shit," I huffed out a laugh. "Does she have any copies of her books at home? Could I maybe get a signed book as a gift for someone?"

Lincoln stopped in the middle of the parking lot. "Mac, no."

I turned back to look at him. "What?"

"I know what you're doing, dude."

Wes looked back and forth between me and Lincoln. "Okay, I'm missing something. Who wants to clue me in?" His eyes landed on me, and I watched them widen as realization dawned on him. "Are you seeing someone?"

"Not really. It's just for a friend."

"Where does your friend live, Mac?" Lincoln questioned me with accusations heavy in his voice. This motherfucker didn't miss a single thing. He had vouched for me before when Nico jumped down my throat, but that nice side of his was clearly gone.

I hesitated too long and he shook his head.

"Juliette."

"Who's that?" Wes asked with a look of confusion washing over his expression. "Wait, is that Coach Anderson's daughter?"

I groaned and ran a frustrated hand down my face. "Fine. Yes, it's for her."

"Bro. You weren't supposed to get attached, remember?"

I glared at him. "Who the hell said I was attached?"

"Did you fuck her?" Wes chimed in with amusement dancing in his eyes.

"Fuck you, Cole."

Lincoln's eyes widened. "Oh my god. You did. And now you're in love with her."

"You're insane," I said, laughing off his words. "She

likes to read. Fucking sue me for wanting to get her a book."

"Okay, but just listen," Lincoln started as he began to walk again. Wes stepped over to his car. "You said if you fucked her, you wouldn't get caught. If you end up getting attached to her, she becomes a liability. Are you following what I'm saying?"

I stared at him for a moment. "So, by giving her a book, I'm somehow going to shoot myself in the foot?"

Wes unlocked his car, deciding to dip out of the conversation. "On second thought, I think I'd rather deal with Charlotte's wrath right now. If you need a book, let me know."

"Not helping, Cole," Lincoln grumbled as Wes simply smiled and got into his car. Lincoln turned back to me. "Do whatever you want, Mac. It doesn't change anything between you and me. I just don't want to see you have your career in jeopardy because you can't keep your dick in your pants."

We both paused, glancing to the right as Wes pulled his car out of his parking spot and beeped at us before he drove out of the lot. I was a bit jealous of him. I wasn't so sure I wanted to go get drinks with Lincoln if he was going to try to be the voice of reason I didn't need.

"I didn't sleep with her and if I did, it doesn't matter. We're just friends."

Lincoln shook his head. "Lie to yourself all you

want, Mac. Just be careful, okay? You're not stupid, even if you are being an idiot right now."

"There's nothing to worry about," I told him dismissively as I tried to divert the conversation away from Juliette. "Now, are we going to go get drinks or are we going to stand in the parking lot for you to continue scolding me?"

"I won't bring it up again," Lincoln promised, holding up his fingers like a Boy Scout.

"That's the best thing you've said all night."

Lincoln rolled his eyes at me. "I'll meet you at Mirage."

"The club?"

A sinister smirk pulled on his lips. "Yep. We're going to find you someone else to occupy your time with instead of our coach's daughter."

"So, Lincoln told me that you guys play hockey together?"

I spun my drink in my hand on the bar and turned to Mia, the girl with black hair sitting next to me. She was friends with the girl Lincoln was talking to. I glanced at him over her shoulder and he nodded.

"Yeah," I said, not giving much more than that. I wasn't really paying attention to anything she was saying the entire time she was sitting beside me.

Instead, I kept downing glasses of vodka and Sprite, regretting following Lincoln here.

Mia grabbed my arm and I instantly pulled it back. My gaze flashed to hers and her eyes were warm as she studied me. "Look, I can tell when someone isn't interested, especially when I'm feeling the same exact way," she said with a laugh. "Clearly, both of our friends had ideas for us that aren't working out."

I tilted my head to the side, my eyebrows scrunching. "Wait, really?"

She nodded and pursed her lips. "She thinks I need to get over my ex, but she doesn't know that I've been talking to him again. I'm just trying to play wingman to appease her, but have no intentions of actually hooking up or talking to anyone."

"Oh, thank God." I let out a breath of relief. I glanced around the room. "Did you drive here?"

A look of confusion filled Mia's expression. "Yeah, why?"

"What do you say we get out of here?" I asked her with a smirk and a wink. "Except, we just go our separate ways and let them think whatever they want to think."

"What happens when she asks me about it tomorrow?"

I shrugged. "Tell her the truth then."

A smile pulled on her lips. "Perfect."

I got out of my seat and walked behind Lincoln, grabbing his shoulder. "We're gonna get out of here."

Lincoln raised an eyebrow. "Oh yeah? Have fun then."

"You too, man."

Mia linked her arm through mine and we headed through the crowd of people inside the club. "You're a genius, Mac."

"I know," I said with a smile as I looked down at her. "Now, let's get you to your car and we can both be on our way."

And I can be on my way home to Juliette.

CHAPTER FOURTEEN
JULIETTE

Sitting in the bathtub, I slowly lifted my glass of wine to my lips, taking a long sip as I soaked in the bubbles. The water was growing cold so I lifted my foot to turn on the faucet to warm it back up. I listened to the sound of the running water as it began to fill the tub even higher. The bubbles stopped just above my chest. I scooted back farther to lift my head higher as it began to fill close to my chin.

I turned the water off again after it reached a comfortable temperature and threatened to spill out onto the bathroom floor. Tonight was a night off from hockey practice, so all I had was work earlier in the day. It wasn't enough to keep my mind distracted.

I couldn't help myself as my thoughts continuously drifted back to Mac and what happened between us last night. Sleeping with him was never part of my plan. Hell, there wasn't a part of Mac that was in my plan. I didn't regret it, but I knew I had made a mistake. He was not someone I was ever supposed to get involved with, which was exactly why I had no intentions of doing that.

Sleeping with someone and getting involved with them were two completely different concepts.

We could fuck without getting attached. I didn't need him to take me to dinner or take me out on dates. Really, I didn't need anything from him, but that didn't change the fact that there was a part of me that wanted him. He was fun… and he was good in bed.

It wasn't necessarily a bad thing. If we kept things superficial and didn't let it go any further than that, we would be golden.

In a way, we were using each other, but if we were in agreement with it, there was nothing wrong. I told him what I wanted from him when I left, and Mac didn't argue with it. He agreed. He wasn't looking for a relationship. He wasn't looking for anything more than someone to occupy his time with and make him come on occasion.

He wanted to be friends with benefits. I wasn't even sure I wanted to be his friend, but life was about compromises. I could be his friend, as long as there was a repeat of last night.

After soaking in the tub a little while longer, I finished my glass of wine and drained the water while I climbed out. Just as I was wrapping my towel around my damp body, my doorbell rang. My gaze met the mirror and I stared back at myself for a moment. Reaching up, I pulled the other towel away from my head and let my hair fall down my back in long natural waves.

It was late at night—far too late for someone to be ringing my doorbell. My footsteps were light as I padded through my condo across the hardwood floors, making a mental note that I needed to get myself a dog. Sometimes being alone made me nervous, especially in instances like this.

I held my phone in my hand, ready to make a call if I needed to as I reached my door. Lifting up onto my toes, I peered through the peephole to see who my uninvited guest was. Relief flooded me and I let out a sigh as I saw him standing on the other side.

Mac Sullivan.

And I was standing here in a damn towel.

A blush was already creeping across my cheeks as I opened the door—as if the man hadn't already seen me naked. His eyes darkened and mischief danced within his irises as he looked me up and down.

"Well, this was unexpected."

I stared at him. "So was your visit."

He smirked. "If I remember correctly, I believe the first time we met, I was only wearing a towel as well."

He was under my damn skin and I wasn't sure if I loved it or hated it.

"What do you want, Mac?"

He tucked his hands into the front pockets of his

jeans. "Nothing in particular," he said with a shrug as he swayed a bit. "I was coming home and thought I'd see if you were awake."

"Did you need something?" I asked him, shifting my weight nervously on my feet.

"Other than you, no."

A fire was burning deep within his gaze and I knew I couldn't entertain it. Not tonight. I needed some space, some time to think. The last thing I was going to do was allow myself to become attached to him. He played for the damn team my father coached. It was a recipe for disaster.

"It's late, Mac."

He stared at me, the playfulness falling from his eyes, and he lifted a hand and grabbed onto the doorway as he continued to burn holes through my own eyes. His face was close enough to mine that I could feel the warmth of his breath as it skated across my skin. A shiver slid up my spine, goosebumps spreading across my arms and legs. I resisted the urge to reach for him.

"Lincoln made me go to the club with him tonight. He was meeting this girl there and introduced me to her friend."

His words sunk into my flesh and my gaze hardened as I looked at him. The goosebumps quickly dissipated and the chill he gave me was replaced with anger. Red-hot jealousy—a foreign feeling.

"Congratulations," I told him with a bored tone. "I

hope you had a great time. If you'll excuse me, I'd like to get ready for bed," I said as I began to shut the door.

Mac pushed out his foot, holding the door open as he shook his head. "They were trying to set the two of us up together. Lincoln thought she'd be someone I would be interested in."

I raised an eyebrow as I crossed my arms over my chest. "Cool. I don't care, Mac."

"I think you do," he said quietly as his eyes did a slow search of mine. It was clear that he was tipsy with the way his words slurred ever so slightly. "I went with him and I met this woman and felt absolutely nothing. And do you know why that is?"

"No," I said softly, not fully trusting my voice. My guard was slipping, but I was desperate to hear what he had to say.

"Because you're the only person I'm interested in, Juliette."

His words replaced the ones that had made me feel jealous. He went and met some other girl, but I was the one who was on his mind. He didn't go home with her. He came back here and came straight to my door. I needed to give myself a reality check before I did something stupid like invite him inside.

"You're drunk," I retorted, attempting to divert the conversation. "And we're just friends."

"Maybe, but that doesn't really change anything, does it?"

I was still wearing nothing but a towel. It was hard

to tell if Mac was using the door to hold himself up or if he was doing it just to make his actions match his words. My lips parted slightly and I didn't trust myself to answer him. Drunken words supposedly spoke sober truths.

Did it change anything?

We were simply just friends and he wasn't interested in anyone other than me.

He wasn't asking for my hand in marriage—or a relationship, even. He was taking a stand and making himself clear, and I fucking heard him. Every single word he spoke.

Mac pushed away from the doorframe with that damn smirk pulling on his lips yet again. "I'll let you go get some sleep," he said with a lightness in his tone. "I just wanted to see you. I wanted you to know."

"Thank you for telling me," I responded, instantly feeling stupid, but also feeling off-balance. Usually I was quick to have some type of a comeback. Something snarky, something witty. I was at a loss for words.

"Good night, Juliette," he said quietly before turning to head across the hall to his condo. I stood in the doorway in nothing but a towel as I watched him unlock his door. The silence was heavy and the air between us was thick with tension. I thought last night would have eased some of the tension, but it was almost as if the sex only made it grow tenfold in intensity.

Thor greeted Mac as he opened his door, and I

watched as his face lit up. He mumbled something to the dog before half stumbling into his home. Just as he was about to shut the door, he glanced over his shoulder at me. His expression was unreadable and the smile from just moments before had since vanished. Instead, the flames were back. The fire was burning fiercely within. He gazed at me for another moment before disappearing into his condo, softly shutting the door behind him.

Turning around, I went back into my own home, locking myself inside. I didn't want to feel, but Mac was relentless. He was making me feel things, and I wasn't sure what to do about it. But there was one thing I was sure of…

Mac Sullivan was going to be my undoing.

And there was nothing I could do to stop it from happening.

CHAPTER FIFTEEN
MAC

Frustration was deep-seated inside my bones as I followed Lincoln down the tunnel toward the ice. It had been over two weeks since I stumbled over to Juliette's condo after going out to the club with Lincoln. There was a part of me that regretted it, so I felt compelled to pull away from her. I didn't want to give her the wrong idea.

We were having fun and I was fairly certain I went and fucked that up by letting it look like I had feelings for her. There was no reason for me to even tell her that I went out and Lincoln tried to set me up with someone else—not that the other woman even mattered. I wanted nothing to do with her. The only person I wanted anything to do with was Juliette.

I didn't know how she managed to do it, but she was rather successful at avoiding me at all costs. I finally caved and texted her two nights ago. She wasn't very forthcoming or warm with any of her responses. Instead, she was short, giving me the briefest answers before telling me she was turning in for the night and would talk to me again soon.

I never heard from her after that and I didn't press the issue.

Not yet, at least.

Juliette didn't strike me as someone who scared easily, but I also knew she was the type to always have one foot out the door. If there was something she didn't like, something that made her uncomfortable, she wasn't going to entertain it.

She tried to make it seem like she didn't care when I confided in her two weeks ago, but her face betrayed her—as did her voice. She told me she didn't care, but I could tell that she did. The way jealousy filled her eyes. The way her tone changed when she admitted she didn't know why I felt nothing for the other woman.

She was trying to protect herself, and I couldn't fault her for that. There was a reason for that, though… Juliette had her own feelings she didn't want to share. Hell, I would be willing to bet she didn't want to even acknowledge that they were real. This girl was going to avoid me until she couldn't anymore and I knew I had to wait it out. I had to let her come to me.

But how long would it take before my resolve broke?

We all filed out onto the ice, each of us skating off in a different direction on our half of the ice as we began to warm up for the game. I watched Nico and Wes as they skated over to the bench where Harper and Charlotte were standing. They came to most of our games. Discontentment pricked at my skin. I was envious of what they had, even if I didn't want it for myself.

"That's not a good look on you, Macky Boy," Lincoln said softly as he skated over to me, shifting his hips as he abruptly dug his edges into the ice and came to a halt, spraying snow as he did so.

I looked over at him as I toyed with my glove like there was something wrong with it, directing my focus to it. "I don't know what you're talking about."

"I know you didn't go home with Mia," he said as he began to skate backward with me moving forward. "Mia told me the two of you bailed. You went home to Anderson's daughter, didn't you?"

"It doesn't matter," I told him with a shrug of indifference as I attempted to brush it off. "That ship has sailed."

The lie tasted bitter on my tongue, but I ignored it. Lincoln didn't need to know that Juliette was occupying every single one of my fucking thoughts. If he knew how she had situated herself under my skin, he wouldn't have approved. The less he knew, the better. Fuck, it was something no one should have even known about.

"Oh, really?" Lincoln prodded, cocking an eyebrow as he grabbed a puck with the toe of his stick and spun around to skate forward. "Why is she over there behind the bench then?"

His words hit me unexpectedly. Whipping my head to the side, I gave myself away, my heart pounding erratically in my chest as I looked over to the bench. Sure enough, there was Juliette, sitting in the row directly behind it. It was the first I had ever seen her show up to a game. Perhaps her father had invited her.

A smile pulled on my lips as I scanned her from where I was standing on the ice. Her hair was hanging in soft waves, framing her face. She had a white turtle neck beneath the Orchid City Vipers jersey she was wearing.

"What's she doing here?" I said quietly as I began to turn away. Lincoln caught my eye, overhearing the words I mumbled to myself.

He tilted his head to the side. "You didn't invite her?"

I shook my head. "I haven't talked to her in, like, two weeks. I don't know what she's doing here."

Lincoln smiled. "I guess you'll just have to find out."

"Are you encouraging me to break the rules, Matthews?"

He shrugged. "I know nothing about what you do. I just know you're not dumb enough to get caught doing it."

"Fair enough."

"Are you two going to get your heads out of your asses and maybe actually fucking warm up with the rest of the team?" Nico yelled at us from where he was in line as everyone started taking shots on our goalie.

Lincoln looked over at me and rolled his eyes before skating off to where the rest of the guys were. Chancing a glance back in her direction, I looked back to Juliette and caught her staring. The corners of my mouth lifted as she quickly diverted her gaze over to the other side of the arena, tearing her eyes from me when she knew she had been caught.

A soft laugh escaped me and I shook my head as I headed over to grab a puck. We ran through our warm-up and it was soon time for us to head back down the tunnel so they could cut the ice again before the game. I skated over toward the bench to get a drink but I didn't dare look at her. Not right now… not yet.

Standing on the ice, I leaned over the boards and grabbed one of the water bottles. I tipped my head back, squirting some into my mouth before wiping away the droplets of water with the sleeve of my jersey. As I straightened my neck, I stared straight ahead at Juliette. She was already watching me and this time, she didn't look away.

She leveled her gaze on mine and I was locked in on her. Everything around me faded into the background. I watched her lips as they slowly pulled into a smile. A blush crept across her face and my throat bobbed as I swallowed roughly.

Fuck.

Everyone was beginning to crowd around the bench

and I quickly hopped over the boards. I stepped over the bench and my lips parted as I went to talk to her through the glass.

"What brings you to a hockey game tonight?"

Juliette stared at me for a moment, her eyes slightly wide. "My father invited me. He thought it would be good for me to come watch one."

I laughed softly and nodded. "Ah, so you're just here because Daddy invited you? No other reason?"

Mischief danced in her eyes and fuck me for missing that look. Juliette shook her head. "Nope, no other reason."

She was toying with me, and I fucking loved it. Not seeing her for two whole weeks felt like pure torture. I knew she was avoiding me, but none of that even mattered anymore. She was here, right in front of me, smiling at me like the sun shined out of my fucking ass. I would take whatever I could get from her, even if she was off-limits to me.

Lincoln grabbed my arm. "Yo, let's go."

I looked over at him and realized that the rest of the team had cleared out and he was waiting for me to head back into the locker room with him. Turning my head, my gaze met Juliette's once again.

"Run along." She laughed, waving her hand, motioning for me to go. "Looks like you have a little game to play."

"Don't worry, baby, I play to impress."

"We'll see about that," she replied with amusement

and not a single ounce of disbelief.

"Mac Sullivan," Lincoln practically yelled at me. "Now."

I winked at Juliette before turning my back to her to follow after Lincoln. We were the last two and right before we reached the locker room, Lincoln abruptly stopped. I collided into his back, a huff of air escaping me as he spun around, stepping into my space. He had me cornered where no one else could see or hear us.

"Dude, what the fuck was that?" His voice was low and harsh, lacking his usual playfulness.

I let out a deep breath, shaking my head. "I don't know, man. I couldn't help myself."

"Do you want to give everyone a reason to be suspicious?" He paused, his eyes boring holes through mine. "You need to get it together, Mac."

He was right. I needed to get my shit together. I couldn't be openly talking to her in public like that unless I wanted someone to ask questions. Hell, Lincoln, Wes, and Nico already knew more than they should have. I could trust the three of them not to say anything to anyone about it, but still. It was risky and I was not treading lightly.

"I fucking know," I told him, the frustration heavy in my tone. I pushed him away from me and took a step toward him. "Is it really that big of a deal, though? She's my neighbor, so we know each other because of that."

Lincoln ran a frustrated hand through his hair. "You

know what, fuck it. You go ahead and do what you want. I have your back regardless, but when you slip up, that's on you. I can't protect you then."

"I don't need you to protect me." I paused and collected myself, trying to understand where he was coming from. "I appreciate you looking out for me, I really do. I'll be more careful."

Lincoln huffed out another breath just as the guys started to come back toward us. The sound of the announcer from the arena began to echo down the hall. "Jesus, take the wheel."

"What wheel is Jesus taking now?" Wes asked as he walked over to the two of us. "I don't think the guy has enough hands for all the wheels we've been handing over to him."

I tilted my head to the side. "What?"

"Did you get dropped on your head as a baby?" Lincoln asked him. Both of our facial expressions matched with our eyebrows pinched and eyes narrowed.

"Cole, Sullivan, and Matthews!" Coach Anderson called from where he was standing. "Stop gossiping and get the fuck out there!"

Shit.

The three of us separated and we all began to file back down the tunnel to the arena. The last thing I needed was to be on Coach Anderson's shit list…

Especially because there was a chance I'd be begging him for forgiveness in the future.

CHAPTER SIXTEEN
JULIETTE

I settled back in my seat, looking out through the glass as the players got into position on the ice. It was the first professional hockey game I had been to in quite some time and it was my first in Orchid City. My father had been bothering me about coming to a game and I finally caved. I knew how much it meant to him for me to come and watch. There was a lingering sadness coupled with a touch of jealousy as I watched the puck drop and hit the ice.

Times like this were when I really felt the loss. It was part of the reason why I avoided coming to any games. It was a different experience watching the kids that I was coaching rather than watching professionals playing at a much higher level. I missed the competitiveness of it. The aggression. The fast pace. There wasn't a single part of it I didn't miss.

I pushed away the feelings of sadness as Lyla

returned to her seat next to me. I wasn't going to let my emotions bring me down anymore. I couldn't, or it was going to destroy me. It had already caused so much turmoil in my life, and it wasn't worth it anymore. I deserved to find some shred of happiness, regardless of how my future looked.

"That line was absolutely insane," Lyla huffed as she handed me a hard seltzer. "I thought I was going to miss the whole game waiting there."

I laughed softly and took a sip before setting it in the cupholder in front of me. "I told you I would have waited for them so you wouldn't miss anything."

Lyla waved her hand at me. "Girl, I don't understand the first thing about this sport. I'm just here because it sounded like a good time. Plus, I heard there are a lot of hot hockey players, and your girl here is a single Pringle."

"Trust me, you don't want any of these guys," I told her as I stared at the backs of their jerseys in front of me. I spotted Mac toward the end of the left side of the bench. Sullivan. Number 13. "They are arrogant grown children with inflated egos and they all smell."

I could feel Lyla's gaze on the side of my face and she shrugged when I directed my attention back to her. "I never said I liked good guys."

We stared at each other for a second before we both busted out laughing. Lyla never ceased to surprise me. When I met her that first day of orientation, she appeared to be this innocent little creature. She had a habit of apologizing for being outgoing and rambling. After I assured her that she didn't have to apologize, that I just wanted her to be herself, she didn't bother holding back.

I learned quickly that when she let her guard down, she didn't have much of a filter. She also wasn't this innocent little person like she appeared to be. Turned out, she had quite the wild side. We had only hung out a handful of times, but Lyla was more of an open book than I thought she would be. And she liked to have a good time, and that was the kind of positivity I needed in my life.

"We have a lot of catching up to do. Since you left the hospital, I feel like I have no idea what is going on in your life."

I shrugged. "There's not much to tell. I've been busy at the rink with my new position there and with coaching."

"Do you miss working at the hospital at all? I know you said it wasn't really what you enjoyed doing," she said as she looked back out at the ice. Her eyes followed the play as it moved down toward the opposing team's goal. "How the hell do they follow the puck? It moves so quickly, I feel like I keep losing track of it."

Laughing, I shook my head. "It's just almost second nature. You learn to follow the movement and your body kind of moves on autopilot. There are definitely times when things happen so fast that the players even miss it." I paused before touching her first question.

"And I don't really miss the hospital, honestly. I'm really happy with what I'm doing now. I always wanted a career in hockey, so it works for me."

"You said you used to play, right?"

I nodded. "I started playing when I could walk. My dad got me into it as soon as he could and when he realized how passionate I was about it, my parents ran full speed with it." I took a sip of my drink and my eyes followed Mac as he climbed over the boards and headed out onto the ice for his next shift. "I was playing at a very high level in juniors and college in the hope of going further. But then I made a stupid mistake that ended my career."

Lyla looked over at me with a touch of sadness in her eyes. "Was it something bad?"

"I got in a car with someone who was driving drunk. We got into an accident, and that's basically the end of the story." I cut it off short, not wanting to go into the painful details. That trip down memory lane wasn't one I liked to do often and even though Lyla was empathetic, she wouldn't fully understand it.

"Damn, that really sucks," she said with a solemness laced within her words. Her eyes filled with pity and it was the exact look I tried to avoid from people. It was the most common response when they heard the story. "I'm sorry that happened to you."

An exasperated sigh escaped me and I forced a smile onto my face. "It's fine," I dismissed. The conversation needed to head in a different direction. "I'm finally starting to feel happy with what I'm doing now. I get time on the ice, I get to work a job around the sport I love, and I get the perks of coming to games like this."

We both turned our attention back to the ice as Mac slammed one of the other players into the boards. The glass rattled and he stole the puck before skating in the direction of their net. I rose to my feet, Lyla following suit as we watched Mac pass the puck to Nico Cirone. Mac moved off to the right side of the net, receiving a pass back from Nico before sending it right over the goalie's shin pads and into the net.

Everyone jumped to their feet as the crowd grew loud. The horn echoed throughout the arena as everyone cheered and high-fived the people around them. Mac celebrated with the guys on the ice before skating past the bench, dapping everyone's gloves.

"Tell me which ones are single. You have to have some kind of insider information on these guys." Lyla's eyes were scanning the bench and I watched her look at Mac as he climbed back over the boards. He glanced over his shoulder, his eyes meeting mine as he flashed both of us a smile. "Oh my. Now who is he?"

Heat crept up my neck before rapidly spreading across my cheeks. The butterflies in my stomach fluttered while my heart threatened to pound through my rib cage. Lyla's eyes widened slightly as she saw my reaction. I tried to recover from it, but my attempt was feeble. "That's Mac Sullivan."

"Goddamn, he's fine," she said with a slow grin

spreading across her lips. "But judging by the look on your face, I'm guessing you agree with me on that one."

Clearing my throat, I shrugged. "He's my neighbor, so we're acquainted."

And he's seen me naked and has been inside me.

"He's your neighbor and you haven't mentioned him once?" She paused for a second. "Let me guess. He either has a girlfriend or he's a complete douchebag."

I couldn't help but laugh, but the laugh came out as a choking, coughing sound. I needed to get my damn self together here. "He's not a douchebag, but he's no different from the rest of them. The ones that are single all tend to be exactly as you would imagine a professional athlete to be with women."

"Ah," she said with a knowing look and a nod as we both settled into our seats. "I'm guessing a playboy. The type who isn't really looking for anything serious, until they find that one girl who changes everything for them and then they finally settle down."

I mulled over her words for a moment. She wasn't wrong with the conclusion she had drawn. I'd grown up around guys like this. Guys that were exactly as she was describing. And there was so much truth to it. They always fucked around with different girls and then out of nowhere, they'd meet one who they decided to settle down with.

That was never in the cards for me. I was never one of those girls that ended up being the chosen one. My ex in college made that abundantly clear. He played hockey too, but we went to separate schools. The long distance wasn't easy and after my accident, things only ended up getting worse.

I wasn't the girl he wanted to settle down with.

And now he was married to the girl he started dating after me.

I would never be someone's endgame.

"I'm not really looking for anything serious, so a guy like that would be perfect," Lyla chimed in, breaking through my muddled thoughts. I quickly pushed them away, my attention back on Lyla. That stupid feeling filled me again as I thought about her and Mac. The same one I felt when I found out he met up with some girl at the club that one night.

Jealousy.

"Trust me, you don't want anything to do with Mac. He's not really your type," I added for good measure, attempting to keep my voice even without the envy creeping in.

Lyla tilted her head to the side, mischief dancing in her eyes as she looked back at the bench. "You know what, I think you're right."

My gaze trailed after hers and collided with Mac's. The play had stopped because of a penalty that I missed, and he was standing on the other side of the bench. His helmet was off and he pushed his damp tousled hair back as he stared at me with a half-smile.

"I don't really go for guys who have their sights set on someone else."

I watched Mac skate back to the center of the ice before looking at Lyla again. "What do you mean?"

She laughed, shaking her head before downing a mouthful of her drink. "Girl, I know you're not blind… or stupid, for that matter."

"I don't know what you're talking about," I lied, pretending like I had no idea what she was saying.

"It's so obvious, Juliette. Look at the way he looks at you," she said pointedly. "That man sees no one but you."

It was my turn to laugh and I half snorted while rolling my eyes. "Please, Lyla. It's nothing. He's my neighbor, nothing more."

She gave me a look that clearly said she didn't believe me. "Whatever you say, Jules."

"Seriously," I insisted, trying to convince her otherwise. "With my dad being his coach, that's just a scandal waiting to happen."

Lyla gave me a devious smirk. "You know, it's only a scandal if you get caught."

"You're like the devil on my shoulder right now," I told her, laughter spilling from my lips. She was not helping at all, especially when I had already broken my vow of silence by speaking to him tonight.

Lyla shrugged with a look of innocence written across her expression. "Hey… all I'm saying is, he's hot and he's clearly into you. Wouldn't it be fun to just live a little instead of constantly having your guard up?"

Mulling over her words again, we both tuned back

into the game. She was right and wrong. I could keep my guard up, but I could still live a little. I could still have fun with Mac and not let him in. And I wouldn't have minded having a repeat of what happened between us the other night.

I stared out at the ice where Mac maneuvered the puck down the ice. As he reached one of the defenders of the other team, he dragged the puck with the toe of his stick, pulling it towards him. He dodged the player and passed it to Lincoln, who shot the puck at the net. Goal.

"Goddamn that was nice," I muttered under my breath, partially in awe as I turned to look at Lyla. "Did you see that toe drag?"

She stared at me in complete confusion. "The what?"

"His toe drag," I explained like the two words had any meaning to her. I sat up straighter in my seat. "You didn't see the way he handled the puck with the toe of his stick before passing it to Lincoln? It was so smooth and looked effortless."

"Look at how excited you are right now," she laughed as a playful smirk danced across her lips. "His toe drags totally make your toes curl."

I couldn't help myself as I laughed out loud. "You're absolutely ridiculous."

"But I'm ridiculously right," she chuckled before taking a sip of her drink. "Girl, please have your fun with that man."

I looked back at the ice as Mac hopped the boards and sat back down on the bench. "I think I might have to."

It was a win-win situation, really. We could have our fun and go our separate ways, and neither of us would get hurt. My heart wouldn't get broken and his career wouldn't be in jeopardy. It was a foolproof plan.

Too bad things never did seem to go as planned…

CHAPTER SEVENTEEN
MAC

Pulling my hoodie over my head, I turned and looked back at Lincoln who was sliding his feet into his sneakers. Wes and Nico had both already headed out, but a few of the other guys were talking about going out and celebrating our win tonight. Lincoln stood up, his gaze meeting mine.

"You're coming out tonight, right?"

I stared at him for a moment, narrowing my eyes the slightest bit. "That depends on if you're going to try to set me up with someone again."

Lincoln half rolled his eyes as he grabbed his cap and pushed his hair away from his forehead as he put it on. "Nope, that won't be happening again. You're on your own now."

"I mean, in all fairness, I never did ask for your help," I reminded him as we both walked out of the locker room and began to make our way out of the building.

"No, and clearly you're going to do what you want anyways." Lincoln paused as he held the door open for me and we fell back into step with one another as we walked to our cars. "Actually… you should invite her and her friend out tonight."

Abruptly coming to a halt, I whipped my head to the side to look at him as he reached for his car door. "What?"

Lincoln glanced at me and shrugged. "Like you said, the two of you are just neighbors. Is there any harm in her and her friend showing up?"

I mulled over his suggestion for a moment. It was a little unexpected coming from him, especially after he practically ripped me a new asshole earlier for being an idiot. Inviting Juliette and her friend came with great risk, unless it was played off like it was just a coincidence. Perhaps Juliette and her friend ended up going to the same place we were going to be at. Perhaps we just accidentally ran into one another.

No one would ever know.

"I can't invite her," I told him, watching as he opened the car door and lowered himself inside. "If I invite her, it's too suspicious."

"You're right," he said with a thoughtful nod. A smirk slowly crept onto his lips. "You could always tell her where you're going to be."

I tilted my head to the side. "I technically wouldn't be inviting her to come along."

"Nope," Lincoln said with a look of indifference and a shrug. "If she ends up showing up there, then it's purely a coincidence."

A smile lifted the corners of my lips. "I enjoy coincidences."

"Tell her to bring her friend along." Lincoln laughed while starting the engine of his car. "I'll meet you at Mirage."

He closed the door without another word and I walked around the front of his car as I made my way over to mine. I wasn't really one who cared for clubs, but when everyone was going out to celebrate a win, it was hard to not go along for the fun. I got in my car, feeling the hum of the engine as I started it. Reaching into my pocket, I pulled out my phone and went to my messages, opening up the text thread between Juliette and I.

MAC

> A bunch of us are heading to Mirage tonight.

I stared at my phone, watching the three bubbles appear as she typed her response.

JULIETTE

> And you're telling me because...

> **MAC**
> In case you and your friend decided to go out tonight. It would be pretty convenient if we ended up at the same place.

She knew what was at stake. She knew what the risks were. Juliette would be safe if anything between us went sideways. If anyone were to find out, she would be the one who walked away unscathed. That was enough assurance for me to gamble with my future.

> **JULIETTE**
> Are you interested in her?

I read her message a second time as I stifled a laugh. "What the hell?" Confusion was evident in my voice, even though she couldn't hear it. I wasn't sure what would have made her think something like that, but if she needed my reassurance, I had no problem giving her that.

> **MAC**
> No, babe. I'm only interested in you.

> **JULIETTE**
> I think we are going out tonight.

> **MAC**
> Maybe I'll see you there.

> **JULIETTE**
> Maybe you will…

A smile was on my lips as I locked my phone screen and slid it into the cupholder. Excitement raced through my veins as I put the car in reverse and finally pulled out of the parking lot. A message came through from Lincoln as I headed down the street, asking where I was. I didn't bother texting him back since it was a short ride into the heart of Orchid City where Mirage was.

I ended up being the last one there, showing up late, which wasn't abnormal. The guys were all sitting in the VIP area, passing around shots when I slid into the booth next to Lincoln. Our win wasn't anything spectacular tonight, but it had basically secured our spot in the playoffs. There were still a few more games until playoffs started, but we were first in our division and we were on a winning streak. There wasn't anything that was going to get in our way.

The thoughts made me nervous and it was something I would never dare to speak out loud. There were certain things that we didn't speak of and definitely never brought up. We all tended to be a little superstitious and the moment something was spoken of was the minute things went sideways.

My eyes surveyed the club as I swallowed back a mouthful of liquor. My throat burned as I chased it down with a sip of water. Juliette gave me no indication of when they would be here, she only left me with a *maybe*. Maybe I would get to see her, but maybe I wouldn't. The ball was in her court now, and it was completely up to her whether or not she made a move.

After a while, I decided I didn't feel like sitting there any longer. There were so many people out on the floor and it was too dim inside. If Juliette were out there, it would have been hard for me to see her from where I was sitting. The guys were deep in conversation about our upcoming trip for some away games, so no one noticed me as I rose to my feet.

I looked out on the dance floor, my heart skipping a beat in my chest the moment I saw her. It was unexpected, but there she was, moving her body to the music, completely unbothered by the people around her. My feet reached the top of the small staircase that led up to the VIP area and I watched her for a moment. Her friend wasn't far from her, but she was dancing with another guy. Juliette's arms were in the air, her hands hanging high above her head. Her long wavy hair hung down her back as she shifted her hips, swaying back and forth with her eyes closed.

This was a side of her I had never seen before. Juliette Anderson came off as if she were uptight and cold. She didn't get close with people unless they were actually important to her. And if there was anyone she didn't like in life, it was most definitely hockey players. I had experienced her frigidness and it was a stark comparison to the Juliette that was dancing by herself right now.

But at the same time, it was also consistent with how she was.

Juliette didn't need anyone—she never did. The only person she needed and the only person she truly trusted was herself.

And I found myself desperate to change that.

My eyes never left her as I headed down the stairs and stepped onto the main floor. I pushed through the crowd, momentarily losing sight of her as a group drifted in front of me. Juliette moved to the side and I saw her again just as there was a break in the sea of people surrounding us. Jesus, she was the most beautiful person I had ever seen. Something about her did something inside me I could never explain. She wasn't supposed to be it for me, but I could feel it in my bones. I just knew…

The air left my lungs in a rush and my feet were cemented to the ground as I continued to watch her. She didn't care about anyone around her. She didn't care about anyone who paused to watch her. She was lost in the moment, just letting herself feel as she let the background noise disappear. There was still so much I didn't know about Juliette Anderson, but as I watched her in that moment it was clear that this was an escape for her.

She was troubled by things she didn't want to talk about, but this—this was good for her. This was just like that night we went skating together.

I wanted to be an escape for her. Hell, I wanted to be her journey and her destination.

My feet began to move and I walked up behind her, pausing with about a foot of space between us. Her perfume invaded my senses and I groaned as I closed the remaining distance separating us. I couldn't help myself. My hands fell onto her hips and I pulled her back flush against me as my face dipped down to her ear.

"What a surprise it is to see you here," I murmured as I traced the shell of her ear with my lips.

Juliette hooked her wrists around the back of my head, moving closer instead of farther away as she continued to shift her hips. I moved with her, swaying along to the beat, feeling her grinding against me. "It took you long enough to come out here."

My hands gripped her hips tighter as my cock throbbed. It was hard as a fucking rock, pressing against her ass as she continued to move to the music. "Were you putting on a show for me?"

"I had to get your attention one way or another," she said as she released the back of my neck and spun around in front of me. My hands slid around to the small of her back and I pulled her into me.

"You always have my attention, Juliette," I breathed, my lips softly brushing against hers.

She grew softer in my arms. Our breaths were mingling together. "Someone might see us, Mac," she reminded me as she threaded her fingers in my hair.

"You think I fucking care?" I murmured as my fingertips dug into her flesh. My mouth captured hers in a bruising kiss. Her lips melted against mine, our tongues tangling. She tasted like strawberries and I couldn't get enough. She was consuming me, drawing me in deeper. There was no way out of this for me, and I wasn't even sure I wanted out anymore.

Juliette broke away, sucking in oxygen. "You should."

"Let them see us, Juliette. Let the whole fucking world know."

It was the truth, even if it was irrational. At that moment, I didn't care. I just wanted her—every damn inch of her—and I was so tired of feeling like I wasn't free to have her.

"Don't be stupid, Mac," she scolded me as she planted her hands against my chest and pushed me away. I half stumbled backward, my eyebrows pulling together as my gaze collided with hers. Mischief danced in her eyes as she reached for my hand and pulled me with her. Next thing I knew, we were wading through the crowd of people. "Come with me."

Those three words were all she needed to say to me.

I would have followed her anywhere.

CHAPTER EIGHTEEN
JULIETTE

Mac's fingers were laced with mine, his palm burning against my own. My heart pounded erratically in my chest, thrumming against my rib cage as I led him through the crowded room. No one paid any attention to us as we pushed past people who were lost in the music, lost in the moment, dancing among themselves or with friends or partners.

I should have cared more about what could have happened or what could have come from this, but I didn't. In that moment, the only thing that mattered was Mac and feeling him close to me again. He was quickly becoming a weakness for me. A simple pleasure I couldn't deny myself anymore. I had fought against him as much as I could.

Now, I didn't have the strength to push him away. Mac Sullivan had successfully broken through the walls

I had carefully constructed around myself. My resolve no longer existed. The power belonged to him and he could do what he wanted with that. If he wanted to destroy me, he could. And at this point, there wasn't a part of me that would have stopped him from trying.

He could destroy me, he could ruin me. If it meant I got to experience these moments with him, I didn't even care. I would deal with the aftermath after the fact. After he was done with me and had decided to move on.

Fuck me for hoping that wouldn't be the case.

I wasn't an idiot, I knew he didn't want a relationship—just like I didn't want one. He played for the team my father coached. There was no way anything between us would ever work out. It was going to be one of those situations where it was fun for the moment but after it was over, we'd be done. There was a part of me that didn't want that, even if I didn't want to actually date Mac.

I just didn't like the idea of him moving on from me. I didn't like the idea of him being with someone else.

There was a hallway off to the side and I pulled Mac along, not knowing what the hell was down there. Mac blindly followed my lead without any questions. It was dark and tucked away, not something someone would see without really looking. With how dark it was, it would have been difficult for anyone to even spot us.

Mac's hand left mine and he grabbed my shoulders as he spun me around to face him. His movements were quick yet calculated. He dropped his hands down to my hips, his fingertips digging into my flesh as he gripped me tightly. His leg pressed between mine, his body enveloping me as he pushed me deeper into the hallway.

"I can't see anything," I murmured as I lifted my hands to hold on to his shoulders. He didn't stop moving us until my back was pressed against the cool wall at the end of the hallway. It could have been a door, I had no clue what it really was, but it didn't matter. The sound of the music wasn't as loud. I could hear him, feel him, and smell him. It was my sight that was at a disadvantage. I could only make out the outline of his body.

It was almost as if there were a glowing halo that was shifting colors around him. It illuminated his silhouette.

"You have other senses other than your sight, Juliette," he murmured as he pressed his mouth against the corner of my lips. I turned my head, seeking him out, but he moved and kissed the other corner of my mouth instead. "Let your other senses take over. Don't worry about what you can or can't see. Feel everything. Hear everything. Fully immerse yourself, Juliette."

He licked my lips.

"And let me fully immerse myself in you."

My mouth instantly went dry. My core tightened as butterflies fluttered within my stomach. Damn this man and the words he spoke. The effect he had on me was maddening. Just another example of how I had zero control and not a single ounce of power here.

It was all Mac.

"You're feeling it all, aren't you?" His voice was soft like silk, sliding against my eardrums as his words tantalized me. His touch was feather-like as his fingertips drifted up my thighs as he began to push up the bottom hem of my dress. A shiver slid down my spine just as he slid his hands beneath the waistband of my panties. "The way your breath just hitched tells me that you are." He was deliberately slow with his movements, kissing me with a tenderness as his tongue slid against mine. "If you take away one sense, it heightens the rest of them."

His mouth left mine, trailing his lips down my neck as he licked and nipped at my skin. Dropping my hands down to the hem of his shirt, I gripped the material and began to push it up his torso. My palms were against the taut muscles on his abdomen, my fingers splayed across his warm flesh. He was extremely fit, which was to be expected, considering he played hockey.

I wasn't shallow, but fuck if I didn't love the way he looked. I loved the way he felt, the way his breath caught in his throat. How his lips found mine in a haste as my fingers dropped down to the waistband of his jeans. He consumed me, breathing me in while his tongue stroked mine. I couldn't think straight with the way he was touching me in the dark.

Nothing mattered except for feeling him, tasting him, experiencing this with *him.*

"Fuck, Juliette," he groaned against my mouth before he broke away from me. I couldn't see what he was doing, but I heard the whoosh of his shirt as he stripped it away from his body and dropped it onto the floor, I presumed. "I fucking need to be inside you."

"How badly?" I murmured as I grabbed the waist of his pants and pulled him back to me. There was an urgency as I began to push the denim, along with his boxer briefs, down his thighs.

Mac slid his hand through my hair, gripping the base of my skull as he jerked it back. "So badly, baby." He grabbed my bottom lip between his teeth, leaving half-moon indents in my flesh before running his tongue over the crescent shapes. "Are you going to let me fuck you right here?"

He didn't make another move as he waited for me to answer. His chest heaved, we were both out of breath already, driven by need and lust. My heart was off-beat as it thumped away in my chest. There was no way to slow it down, not with Mac this close, talking the way he was.

Two could play at that game.

"You would like that, wouldn't you?"

Mac's chest vibrated as he chuckled while slowly releasing my hair. He dragged his hands down the sides of my neck, then across my collarbones, before beginning their descent down my torso. I shivered beneath his touch as the heat spread across my skin like wildfire. The sensation made me feel like I was going to spontaneously combust beneath his touch. There was no one who played my body the way he did and made it a fucking experience like this.

I would never tell him the truth, but there wasn't a single person on this planet that was comparable to Mac Sullivan. He was in a league of his own. It was like his touch was filled with magic. He was the biggest threat I had ever met. And I was walking straight into his arms instead of running in the opposite direction.

"You want me to beg, Jules?" he murmured as he traced the seam of my lips with his tongue. His kiss was rough and demanding as his mouth collided with mine. He breathed me in, drawing the air from my lungs until I was starved of oxygen. Abruptly, he broke away from me. "Just say the words and I'm down on my fucking knees."

Jesus Christ.

My skin was burning and warmth was building within the pit of my stomach without him even being inside me. This was absolutely maddening. I needed him, but this sense of power, this sense of control... The flames licked my veins, urging me to do it. To take it. To tell him exactly what I wanted from him.

"Get on your knees," I said slowly, my voice thick with lust. "Get down on your knees and beg."

Mac let out a low growl, murmuring something I didn't catch as he did exactly what I said. His hands continued to slide down my torso as he lowered himself down onto the floor in front of me. I couldn't see him, except for the outline of the top of his head. I reached for him in the darkness, my hands touching the silky soft waves. I threaded my fingers through them, giving his hair a light tug.

"You're so fucking hot," he said quietly, as he hooked his fingers under the waistband of my panties and began to inch them down my thighs. "Please, Juliette. I need to be inside you. Please let me fuck you. Let me cover your mouth so I can keep you quiet as I fuck you up against this wall."

My insides were melting. If he didn't stop talking soon, I would be a complete puddle at his feet.

"Please let me, baby," he murmured, trailing his lips down my thigh. "Let me have my way with you." He pulled off my shoes and slid my feet through my panties. "I'm begging you, Juliette."

I stared down at him as he continued to kiss the insides of my thighs, working his way back up my body. My grip tightened on his hair as he reached the apex of my thighs.

"Goddamn, look at that pretty pussy," he groaned, running his tongue along my center. "You're so wet and ready for me, aren't you?"

Pulling tighter on his hair, I pulled his face away from my pussy and then reached for his arms to pull him to his feet. "Shut up and fuck me, Mac."

"Gladly." I could hear the smile in his voice as he

rose to his feet. He kissed me in a haste before grabbing my hips and spinning me around to face the smooth surface of the wall. He lowered his mouth to my ear. "I'm not going to be gentle with you and I'm not going to take my time, pretty girl. I'm going to fuck you. Fast and hard."

Dropping one hand from my hip, he spit into his hand. He pumped his cock twice, getting it wet with his saliva before closing the distance between us again. He pushed my chest against the wall, forcing me to turn my head until my cheek was also against the wall. The plaster was cool beneath my skin that was currently caught in an inferno.

His other hand lifted my dress and gripped my hip as he pressed the tip of his cock against my center. He took a moment, sliding it through my arousal before pushing into me. I couldn't stop the moan from falling from my lips as he filled me to the brim. "Oh my god," I breathed as I felt myself stretching around his girth.

"Just breathe, baby." His voice was hoarse and thick with need as he whispered the words into my ear. He pulled out slightly before slowly thrusting back in. "That's it. Take every fucking inch of me."

He grabbed both of my hips and I was up on my toes with our height difference as he bent his knees while he began to move faster. We were still in the dark and the music from the main room was echoing down the hall. No one had come this way yet and even if they did, I wasn't quite sure I would care anymore. I was breathless, a mess of moans as Mac released my hip with one hand and wrapped it around my throat.

"Look at you," he groaned, nipping at my earlobe as he tightened his grip on my throat. His hips worked faster and I pressed back against him, taking his entire length with every thrust. He filled me to the hilt, pumping into me harder. The force of his thrusts shook me to my core and the warmth inside was spilling over the edges, dripping into my veins. "Fuck, you take me so well."

My vision blurred, my legs burned, and my lungs screamed for more oxygen. I was on the precipice of seeing stars and I couldn't tell if it was from my quickly approaching orgasm or his hand wrapped around my throat. Either way, I fucking loved it.

"Don't stop, Mac," I moaned as he loosened his grip around my throat. "I'm so close."

Mac let go of my hip and slid his hand around the front of my body, slipping it down between my legs. His fingers brushed against my clit and I cried out. He released my throat and clasped his hand over my mouth.

"Shh," he murmured as he rocked into me again. "We can't have anyone finding us, remember?"

I nodded my head, my legs turning into fucking Jell-O as he began to fuck me harder. His fingers rolled over my clit repeatedly. My face contorted, my eyes slamming shut as I moaned loudly into his palm. My orgasm hit me without any further warning, the volcano inside me erupting as the heat spread through my body.

"Juliette," Mac breathed my name as he slammed into me again. My pussy clenched around his cock, my legs shaking as he continued to play with my clit as he lost himself inside me. His warmth filled me, his thrusts slowing as he emptied himself deep inside.

We were both breathless, riding the waves of euphoria as he moved his hand away from my mouth and smoothed my hair from my face. He was still inside me, still pinning my body to the wall. The entire club was still moving, just at the end of the dark hallway we were hidden inside. He just fucked me relentlessly, but his touch now was gentle and tender. His lips were soft as he pressed them against my temple.

He sighed, pressing his forehead to where his lips were a moment ago. He lingered for a second before slowly pulling out of me. I could feel his cum dripping down my thigh as he pulled his pants up before crouching down in front of me to smooth my dress.

I slowly turned to face him, pressing my back flush against the cool wall as I watched him pick up my underwear and shoved them into his pocket. A ghost of a smile danced across his lips knowing he had been caught. He moved back into my space and reached out to cup the side of my face. A ragged breath slipped from his lips before he pressed them to mine in a tender kiss.

"I don't know what you're doing to me, Juliette," he

whispered against my lips. "And I'm not sure I want you to stop."

His words shook me to my core, nestling deep within the fibers of my bones. He wasn't alone with his feelings, but I couldn't admit that I felt the same way.

Even if I didn't want either of us to stop this.

CHAPTER NINETEEN
MAC

Following Wes and Nico, we all walked into the front doors of the hotel. I paused for a beat, turning my head as I saw them heading toward the restaurant that was nestled inside. My stomach growled and I sighed before heading in their direction. Lincoln walked up beside me, pushing against my arm with his elbow.

"That was one hell of a game tonight," he exclaimed with a grin as we stopped behind the other guys who were talking to the hostess. He wasn't lying. It was a close one—an extremely competitive one—but we still pulled through and ended up winning. We played well the entire time, but the other team was good. They made it challenging, which honestly made it more fun.

It was the last of our four away games and I was fucking exhausted.

"I'm just ready to get home. I miss my bed and my dog."

Lincoln smirked. "I'd be willing to bet those aren't the only things you're missing."

"Who's watching Thor, anyways?" Wes asked me as we all sat down at the table our hostess led us to. "Charlotte said you didn't ask her this time."

I chewed on the inside of my cheek. There was a college girl who lived in my building that I usually paid to take care of Thor while I was gone if one of the guy's girlfriends couldn't do it. Before I left, Juliette offered and I took her up on it. She was able to take Thor to the rink with her so he didn't have to be by himself. And he had really gotten attached to her.

"Juliette is keeping him at her place, so he's not alone."

It was honestly the best-case scenario. Thor got to actually stay with someone, so that was a little different than someone just stopping in to feed him and taking him out to go to the bathroom. He had actual one-on-one interaction with a human for as much time—if not more—than he would have been getting if I were home. Hell, he was more spoiled with Juliette. Since he went to work with her, he practically had no time by himself.

Judging by the pictures she had sent me with him lying on the couch with her, I think it was safe to say he was happily content. He was well taken care of by her, and it warmed my heart. It also gave me an excuse to talk to Juliette every day, so really, all three of us were winning here.

"Your neighbor?" Nico questioned me with an eyebrow raised. He grabbed a menu from the table in front of him and opened it up. "Anderson's daughter?"

I nodded. "That would be the one."

"That's really nice of her," Wes chimed in with a lopsided grin. There was more behind the smile, but I wasn't going to call him out on it. Wes knew. Nico knew. Lincoln knew. That didn't mean we were going to sit down and have a discussion about it.

"That's cool," Nico said with a shrug of indifference. The small gesture caught me off guard. I expected him to start lecturing me again, but he didn't. "Wes, didn't you have something you wanted to ask everyone?"

The conversation drifted away from Juliette and I. We all stared at Wes for a moment as a nervous expression appeared on his face. He glanced around the table, chuckling to himself as he took a sip of his drink. "Okay, so this is a weird thing to ask, but I'm trying to prove something to someone and I kind of need to win."

Lincoln's brows lifted. "We're listening," he answered for all three of us.

"You guys know Charlotte's brother Leo? There's a big figure skating competition in, like, two weeks in Orchid City. I told Charlotte we would all come out to show our support."

"I don't understand what you're winning here," Nico pointed out as he looked up from his menu.

Wes folded his arms on the table, leaning forward like it was something important. "Leo came to one of our games when I first met Charlotte. We talked about it one night and he bet me that if a bunch of hockey players knew about a figure skating competition, they wouldn't show the same support like he was supposed to when he came to my game. I bet him they would. So, we're all going."

"I'll go," Lincoln shrugged. "I've never been to an actual professional competition, only my sister's competitions when we were younger."

Nico smiled. "Harper already beat you to it, bro. I guess she and Charlotte talked about it and she already told her we would go."

"What about you, Mac?" Wes asked me after he turned his attention away from Nico. "Do you think you'd be able to come?"

"Sure, I'll come along," I told him with a smile. I could tell he was a little uncomfortable asking us, especially since he already told Charlotte we would all be there. We had all met Leo a few times when he was in town and hanging out with Charlotte and Wes. He lived a few hours north in Idyll Cove and didn't visit often. He was also a professional figure skater, so he traveled a lot.

Wes seemed pretty fond of him, though, and he was always cool with me. I had also never gone to an event like that, so it could be fun.

"You should invite Juliette." Lincoln dropped his

voice lower so the words were only spoken between the two of us.

I slowly turned my head to the side to look at him. "Why would I do that? You know we can't be seen together."

"It won't be the two of you together. She'll be hanging out with all of us." He paused for a moment, glancing at Wes and Nico who were talking about the menu. "It would really be a safe place for you guys. You know none of us are going to tell anyone and if someone sees all of us together, they would just see a group of friends hanging out."

I considered his words and pondered over the option. It was a way for the two of us to spend time together without having to do it in hiding. While it was fun sneaking around and making sure no one found out, I also hated it. I wanted to be able to walk around with Juliette and not have to worry about the implications of the two of us being together.

"I'll see what she thinks about it," I told him before looking up at Wes and Nico. "You don't think they will judge or say anything about it?"

Lincoln shook his head and smiled. "I told you bro, we're all your family." He paused and grabbed my shoulder with his hand. "We might all talk shit, but at the end of the day, we're only here to support one another and look out for each other."

Lincoln was right.

At the end of the day, that was exactly what we all were.

Family…

———

The screen on my phone went black for a moment before Juliette's face appeared in front of me. Her face was free of makeup with her hair pulled back in a high ponytail. She stared back at me with her dark gray eyes. Damn, I fucking missed her.

"Hey you."

Juliette smiled, her lips spreading as she flashed her straight white teeth at me. "Hey yourself."

"How was your day?" I asked her as I adjusted on the bed in my hotel room. Most of the guys were still down at the bar, but I snuck away to come up to my room to talk to her. With the time difference, I didn't want to be rude and call her later, even though it was already approaching midnight at home. "How was Thor for you today?"

She brushed her hair away from her face and tucked it behind her ear. Thor must have heard me because his nose came pushing around her and his head took up the screen on my phone. The sound of Juliette's laughter came through the speaker and I saw her face pop up beside Thor's as he licked the side of her face.

"He's on the phone, bud," she told him, scratching the top of his head before he disappeared from my line of sight. "My day went well. It was pretty busy but I got through it. Thor was good. He slept a lot on the floor in my office and then he played with some of the kids at the rink. He was sleeping until he heard the sound of your voice." She paused for a second and the smile fell from her lips. "I think he misses you."

I stared at her for a moment, watching her as her tongue darted out to wet her lips. I should have kept my mouth shut, but I couldn't. Something about Juliette always had me going against my better judgment.

"Is he the only one who misses me?"

Her eyes widened slightly. The shock was evident in her expression. Her throat bobbed as she swallowed hard. There was a pregnant pause and the tension was palpable. I half expected her to change the subject—anything to avoid giving me a real answer.

She gave me exactly what I wanted.

"No, he's not."

The truth.

Juliette wasn't as cold as the ice she skated on. It was all a facade to keep people away. To protect herself. I had stripped the layers away and broken through the walls she had constructed around herself. And I was still a little surprised by what I had found underneath her frigid exterior.

Juliette Anderson was just as gone for me as I was for her.

"I'm ready to come home," I admitted, my voice low as I stretched out onto my back and held my phone above my head. "I'm ready to come home to both of you."

Juliette's eyes were warm. "We're both here waiting for you."

"I should be home by mid-morning tomorrow."

"Did you want me to leave Thor at my place and you can just get him when you get home, or should I take him to work with me?"

"I don't care about my dog right now, Juliette," I laughed, shaking my head at her. It didn't matter if I got him before or after she got home. Either way, she would be seeing me at some point tomorrow, and not just to drop off the damn dog. "I want to see you."

"Good," she said, the corners of her lips lifting upward. "I'll take Thor to the rink with me. You can come by if you want, or I'll just see you after I get home."

"What if I did both?"

She tilted her head to the side. "What do you mean?"

"I'll come to the rink and get him, so you don't have to worry about him, and then I'll come over after you get home."

A playful smirk slid across her lips. Mischief danced in her eyes. "Getting tired of your own company, Sullivan?"

"My hand doesn't feel as good as you do."

She rolled her eyes and snorted as she turned onto her stomach on the bed. The mattress pushed her tits up and my cock twitched in my pants. Goddamn, I missed her in every fucking possible way. "You're ridiculous."

"Only for you, baby."

Juliette laughed and the sound snaked itself around my eardrums. "Just come home, Mac. Your smelly dog and bored neighbor miss you."

I was ready to find my own flight home right now. "You want me to come occupy your time?"

She raised a questioning eyebrow. "Isn't it obvious?"

"It is now."

"Good," she repeated with a satisfied smile. "I'm going to go to sleep, that way it will be morning soon."

I couldn't help but smile back at her. The butterflies in my stomach fluttered and the feeling was something I was still getting used to. No one had the effect on me that Juliette had. It was foreign, but thoroughly enjoyable.

"Before you go, I had something I wanted to ask you."

Curiosity flickered in her gray irises. "Okay."

"Well, it's actually two things," I started as I sat upright in bed. "Wes's girlfriend's brother has a figure skating competition in Orchid City this weekend and I wanted to see if you'd like to come with all of us. Just as friends… you know, so no one would think anything."

She nodded. "Okay. That sounds like it could be fun."

It wasn't a yes or a no, but I needed to keep moving before I got cold feet. I wasn't sure cold feet actually existed where Juliette was concerned. I was more susceptible to getting tongue-tied and fucking up my words trying to talk to her. So, they just all tumbled out like word vomit instead.

"I want to take you out. Just the two of us. We can go somewhere that is a little farther away, that way we don't run the risk of running into anyone. Somewhere we can get dinner and then do something. I don't know. It doesn't have to be a date or anything like that if you don't want it to be."

"Mac," Juliette's voice was soft as she broke through my rambling. "Stop. The answer is yes. I want to go on a date with you."

My eyes widened and my stomach fluttered again. "Wait—you do? It doesn't have to be a date. I don't want you to feel uncomfortable or anything."

She stared at me for a moment and I could feel her gaze reaching deep inside me, like she saw every part of me. "I want it to be a date, Mac." She let out a breath. "Try again."

I inhaled deeply, collecting myself. I didn't know what the hell was going on with my brain right now. It was like it was short-circuiting. Juliette bit back a grin as she waited for me to speak again.

"Will you go out on a date with me, Juliette?"

Her lips widened and she smiled. "I would love to."

I couldn't help but smile back. "Okay, good."

Her eyes shimmered. "It's a date."

"Get some sleep, beautiful," I told her as I glanced at

the clock and realized it was definitely past midnight at home now. "I'll see you tomorrow."

"Until then," she said, still with that same warm smile on her perfectly plump lips. I wanted to reach out and touch them. I wanted to trace them with my tongue before tasting her. "Sweet dreams."

My self-control had officially disappeared.

"I'll be dreaming of you."

Juliette laughed softly. "Good."

"Good night," I told her, not wanting to actually hang up. There was something about her comfort that brought me an intense sense of peace. I wanted to revel in it, to stay suspended in that feeling forever.

"Good night, Mac," she said quietly as she made no move to hang up either. There was hesitation and we both sat there for an elongated breath, staring at one another. A blush crept across her cheeks and she cleared her throat before the screen went black.

Shaking my head to myself, I laughed as I stood up from the bed. Clearly I wasn't the only one who was losing their self-control and ability to function properly. The feelings between us were mutual and that was all I needed. I was going to make sure Juliette never regretted anything that happened between us.

She was already the best thing that had happened to me.

And I wanted to be the same for her.

CHAPTER TWENTY
JULIETTE

Sitting at my desk, I glanced down at Thor where he was lying on the floor by my feet. He lifted his head, looking up at me as his tongue hung out. I reached down and pet the top of his head before turning back to my computer. We had a busy morning and the kids that were here earlier wore him out after their clinic.

It wasn't usually busy during the week until the afternoon but they didn't have school today, so we set up a clinic for them. Thor thoroughly enjoyed all of the kids being here because it gave him some friends to play with, even if they were human. He was very much a people dog and the past week, he had become a staple here.

There was a knock on my door and I called out to whomever it was to tell them they could come in. It was Chase, one of the other coaches who was here for the day. He smiled brightly, laughing as Thor came running over to him. His black hair hung in his face as he bent over and pet him before looking back at me.

"Are you sure you have to give him back?"

I laughed along with him as he stepped farther into my office. He walked to the other side of my desk and sat down in one of the chairs across from me. "Unfortunately, I think his owner would be pretty upset if he didn't get him back."

"He's basically become the rink's mascot. I heard some of the kids talking about wanting their team to be named after him."

"They're funny little people," I said, shaking my head. I moved a stack of papers to the other side of my desk. "I'm sure Thor is going to miss coming here just as much as they are going to miss him."

"Maybe you can still bring him some days?" Chase kind of shrugged, like he wasn't that worried about it, but if it weren't something Chase felt was important, he wouldn't have brought it up. We had spent a lot of time together the past few weeks and from what I had learned about him, he was a pretty straight forward kind of guy. "He's been good for the kids and the morale around here."

I stared at him for a moment before nodding. I looked down at the two forms that were on my desk, my eyes briefly scanning over the fundraiser papers. "I know what you mean. I will see what I can do. His owner might be okay with it, that way Thor isn't stuck at home by himself."

"His owner might be okay with what?"

My head abruptly lifted and I looked past Chase as my gaze collided with Mac's. Thor was already barreling toward him. Mac crouched down to greet his dog, giving him a rough scratch and hug before standing back up. The air left my lungs in a rush and my lips parted as a ragged breath escaped me. "Hey."

"Hey," he smiled at me as he crossed his arms over his chest and leaned against the doorframe. Thor sat down by his feet and pushed his body against Mac's solid thigh. Mac's gaze dropped to the back of Chase's head, his eyebrows drawing together slightly before he looked back at me. "Am I interrupting something?"

Chase turned around, his eyes widening as he realized who Mac was. "Wait, Thor's owner is Mac Sullivan? Why didn't you tell me that?" Chase quickly rose to his feet and walked over to Mac with his hand out. "I'm Chase Odell. I'm one of the coaches here. I was just talking to Jules about how great of a dog Thor is."

Mac shook his hand and smiled before glancing at me. "He is a great dog, isn't he, *Jules*?"

His tone was off. It wasn't his normal warm, playful self. Chase didn't pick up on the shift in him and thought he was being friendly. But I noticed it. It was like there was a thorn stuck in his side. His eyes weren't as soft as they normally were. The muscle in his jaw ticked.

Mac Sullivan was *jealous*.

I stifled a laugh. "He is. We were talking about how great he has been here and whether or not you would let me bring him back."

"My dog isn't for rent," Mac said as he looked down at Thor. Thor was staring out the door, watching a group of kids as they ran past, laughing. His ears perked up and he looked like he wanted to go run with them. "But I would be okay with him getting out of the house when I'm not there."

"Really?" Chase asked him, his face lighting up. "Thanks, man! The kids are going to be so excited to hear that. They thought today was his last day and have a special treat for him."

Mac smiled a genuine smile and nodded. "When I'm at practice and games, Thor is just left by himself. I think it would be good for him and give him something to do." He looked back at me again. "Only if you're okay with toting him along with you."

"Of course," I told him as I pushed my chair away from my desk and straightened my spine. "Thor is never a bother."

"I'll go tell the kids," Chase chimed in before disappearing from my office, leaving Mac and I alone. The lingering tension was still thick in the air and he pushed away from the doorjamb before closing the distance between us in my office.

"Coach Chase seems nice."

I tilted my head to the side, my eyebrows drawing

together as he sank down into the seat across from me. "He is." I sighed with annoyance. "Your insecurities are showing, Sullivan."

There was a cruelness in the smirk that pulled on his lips. "I'm not insecure, baby. I know he can't make you scream his name the way I make you scream mine." He winked. "You're nice to him, so I know you don't have any feelings for him."

"So what is your problem with him then?"

Mac planted his hands on my desk and leaned across the space as his face dipped close to mine. His eyes burned holes through my own. "You're mine, Juliette."

"Excuse me?"

"You heard me," he murmured, his voice low and expression soft. "I'm staking my claim. Marking my territory. Chase Odell needs to know that you're spoken for."

I rose to my feet, inserting my face directly in his. "Chase is not a threat, Mac. And with the way you came in here, I'm sure he got the message."

Mac pushed off the desk and walked around it. I turned around to face him as he reached me. He moved closer, his legs pushing mine backward until my ass hit the wooden desk behind me. Mac's hand slid around the nape of my neck and I tilted my head up to look at him.

"Did *you* get the message?"

My mouth was instantly dry and my tongue darted

out to wet my lips. I watched his gaze drop down to my mouth before moving back at my eyes. "I'm not so sure I did," I told him, my voice barely above a whisper.

A ghost of a smile danced across his lips and his face lowered to mine. "Let me show you instead."

His mouth captured mine, stealing the air from my lungs as he pushed my lips open with his tongue. He wasted no time deepening the kiss as his tongue made contact with my own. My chin lifted higher, giving him more access as he slid his hand around the front of my throat and tightened his grip on me. Our surroundings faded away and he kissed me senseless.

My mind barely registered his hands as they dropped down to my waist and he hoisted me up onto the desk. His body moved closer to mine, my legs parting to let him in. Instinctively, I wrapped my legs around his waist and held him close to me. My hands fisted the front of his t-shirt and his fingers were in my hair, pulling my head back to give him even more access to my mouth.

Our tongues were tangled in their own dance. He was consuming me, surrounding me, pulling me into the depths of him. I was entirely lost in Mac Sullivan and it scared the shit out of me. I kept people at arm's length for a reason, and I could feel myself slipping. There wasn't anything left for me to grab onto except for him. I was falling for him, but I knew I couldn't. I knew it was something I couldn't succumb to.

But that didn't mean I was going to deny myself of

the pleasure that he could give me.

A loud knock on the open door to my office had my body falling rigid. Someone cleared their throat. I pulled back a bit, my chest heaving with every shallow breath I took as I looked at Mac with my eyes wide. His lips were swollen from kissing me, his cheeks flushed. He looked past me and then smiled my way as he took a step back.

"Sorry, I didn't mean to interrupt," Chase said in a nervous tone as I hopped off the desk and turned around to face him. I was a touch embarrassed by the fact that he just walked in on Mac and I making out. The pit of my stomach rolled as I realized that Chase was the only person to see us like this… and he knew my father coached the team Mac played for.

"You're fine, Chase," I laughed nervously as I pulled my hair back into a ponytail. Mac stood back with a look of satisfaction on his face. Chase was clearly uncomfortable, but I knew it was because of what he walked in on, not because he saw me with another guy. Things weren't like that between us. "Did you need something?"

He shifted his weight on his feet. "I actually had a question for Mac," he said before looking past me to him. "The kids heard that you were here and I was wondering if you could spare a few minutes to skate with them. They're getting ready to get on the ice for another skills session, but I also know you're busy and probably need to get going."

I turned around to look at Mac who shook his head. "Actually, my day is pretty wide open. Let me grab my skates, stick, and gloves from my car and I'll meet you guys on the ice."

"Thank you so much," Chase said with such sincerity in his voice. "You have no idea how much it will mean to these kids."

Mac nodded and Chase disappeared out of my office, once again leaving us alone. Mac closed the distance between us and reached up to cup the side of my face. "We're finishing this later, Juliette. Are you free tonight? I want to take you out."

"I am."

Mac's lips met mine in a soft, slow, torturous kiss. "It's a date then."

"I guess it is, isn't it?"

He took a step back before walking around my desk and heading in the direction of the door. He paused in the doorway, turning back to face me. "Come meet us on the ice. I could use a passing partner to demonstrate some stuff for the kids."

My eyes widened slightly. "I'm sure one of the other coaches could go out there with you."

"I don't want them, Juliette," he said simply as he stared at me. "I want you."

He didn't speak another word as he headed out into the hall. I stared at the door where he was last standing, feeling his words as they sank into the fibers of my soul. He was in my veins and I was utterly fucked.

CHAPTER TWENTY-ONE
MAC

"Holy shit, that was so cool."

My eyes widened as I stared down at the little ten-year-old and stifled a laugh. "I don't think you're supposed to be saying those words, bud."

A nervous laugh escaped him and he undid the straps on his helmet before pulling them off. "Please don't tell my mom," he said with a tense smile. "She'll definitely ground me."

I clapped my hand over his shoulder, squeezing the padding underneath. "Don't worry, Jake, I won't say anything."

"This is exactly why you're my favorite player."

"Because I'm not going to tell on you?" I asked him, laughing as I walked with him toward the locker room that the rest of the kids had funneled into.

They were all starstruck when I hit the ice. I assisted

the coaches with the different drills they had the kids doing and showed them some tips that were more at their level. Juliette was able to come out for a few minutes but she ended up getting called away for something business related instead.

I didn't get the chance to see her actually play, but there would be time for that. And I couldn't wait to challenge her on the ice.

"Well, I mean, that's just a bonus on top of how good of a player you are."

I shook my head, still laughing. When I was his age, I never had the chance to meet a professional player so I couldn't have said how I would have acted. He seemed nervous, like he needed to impress me at first, but now he was acting like a normal typical kid. Like I wasn't someone he idolized, even though he made it clear he had me sitting on a pedestal.

"Well, one day I'm sure you'll be giving me a run for my money. You're extremely talented, Jake. If you keep up with it and keep pushing yourself, you'll be going places one day."

His little eyes lit up and his lips parted. "You really think so?"

"Absolutely." I paused for a moment as he put his stick outside of the locker room. "It takes a lot of discipline and hard work, but I believe in you."

"Wow. Thank you, Mac."

"Jake, get in here and get changed," Chase pushed

the door open and called out to him. "Your mother will be here soon."

I held my hand out to shake Jake's. "It was nice meeting you. I hope to see you on the roster for a professional team one day."

"Yes, sir," he said with a swift nod and a firm handshake. I watched him as he turned around and disappeared into the room where the rest of the kids were.

"That was really kind of you, Mac."

I slowly turned around at the sound of Juliette's soft voice. "Is it going to snow? Because that sounded an awful lot like a compliment."

She rolled her eyes and snorted as she bit back a grin. "Would you rather I be mean to you instead?"

Shaking my head, I smiled at her. "As much as I like your fiery attitude, I like you soft for me even more."

"I should be home around six, but I'll need to get a shower and get ready, though."

I nodded and we began to walk toward the coaches' locker room. "You take all the time you need. Do you want to plan on around seven or do you need more time than that?"

"That should be enough time," she agreed, pausing outside the door with me. "I'll see you at seven then."

"Until tonight," I said with a smile before slipping into the locker room to get out of my skates and back into my sneakers. Juliette wasn't in her office when I went up to get Thor, so I left her a note instead.

Wear something comfortable tonight, baby. I'm taking you to get dinner but I have other plans for us.

The rest of the day will drag waiting for you, but you're well worth the wait.

-Mac

I waited until it was seven o'clock on the dot before stepping out of my condo and walking across the hall to Juliette's door. I was wearing a pair of dark charcoal gray pants, along with a white Henley. The sleeves were pushed up to my elbows and I lifted my fist to knock on her door. Thor was less than amused when I left him behind tonight. I think he was a little spoiled having Juliette with him all the time.

Time stretched and I shifted my weight on my feet as I tucked my hands into the front pockets of my pants. After about a minute, I heard the lock on the other side of the door click before Juliette pulled the door open. She was wearing a pair of leggings with an oversized baby blue sweater. It hung down to the center of her thighs. A pair of black boots were on her feet and her hair was pulled back, half up, lying in loose waves down to the center of her back. Her facial features were highlighted by the smallest amount of makeup.

Goddamn, she was fucking beautiful.

"Is this okay?" she asked me as she glanced down at

her feet and back to my eyes. "I can go change if I need to."

I shook my head. "You're perfect, Juliette." I paused, unable to fight the grin that slid across my lips as I allowed my eyes to search her face. "I have one request for part of our date. I need you to grab your stick, skates, and gloves."

She tilted her head to the side. "What do I need those for?"

"You'll see."

Her eyebrows pulled together and she straightened her spine. "Are we going somewhere to play hockey?"

I shrugged with indifference, not wanting to give anything away. "Maybe. Maybe not. I guess you're just going to have to wait and see."

Juliette sighed with a look of irritation, although there was a playfulness in her expression. "You're kind of annoying."

"You like me anyways."

"That's debatable," she retorted, while rolling her eyes. She pushed past me and I inhaled the smell of her perfume as she pulled her door shut behind her. "My stuff is in the car."

A smile touched my lips but I didn't argue with her or attempt to engage in a debate. She could act like that all she wanted—she wasn't fooling anyone. She and I both knew the truth, but if she didn't want to acknowledge it, I would play along.

I followed after her and we stepped into the elevator

together before heading down to the main lobby. We walked out into the parking lot and stopped by her car so she could get her stuff before putting them in my car. Juliette slid into the passenger's side as I closed the trunk and walked around to my side. As I climbed inside, I paused and watched her for a moment as she settled in the seat.

She looked like she was exactly where she belonged.

And I never wanted to see her anywhere but with me.

―――

Juliette looked surprised when I pulled up outside of the French restaurant that was near the rink. She didn't rush out of the car and gave me the chance to open the door for her. I held my hand out to her and she slowly slid her palm against mine as her eyes searched my expression.

"You said what I was wearing was fine," she told me in an accusatory tone. "This place is far too nice for what I'm wearing."

I stifled a laugh and pulled her out of the car, shutting the door behind her. My fingers laced with hers, feeling the warmth of her skin under my touch. She didn't pull away from me. "You look perfect, Juliette. Trust me, it's a nice restaurant, but they don't have a dress code."

"I still feel like I'm underdressed."

I glanced at her as we reached the front door to the stone building. "I come here dressed in sweatpants half the time. You already look better than anyone else. Don't fret, my love."

A pink tint drifted across her cheeks, but the lights were dim enough inside the restaurant that her blush was hidden. I saw it and that was enough for me. I knew the effect I had on her. It was clear she knew it too, even if she wanted to act like she was oblivious to it all.

I gave the hostess my name and she led us through the small space to the table that was reserved for the two of us. It was a booth, tucked away in the corner of the room. Perfect and private, just what I wanted with her.

"This is really nice, Mac," Juliette whispered as she slid into the circular booth. I expected her to put some distance between us, but much to my surprise, she didn't stop moving until she was sitting right beside me. The place settings on the table were arranged that way, but I knew that wasn't why she sat by me. Juliette Anderson had a thing for doing the opposite of what people told her to do, so I didn't see her sitting in the spot expected for her just because it was set up that way.

"I should have asked if you liked French food before assuming you would like it here."

She tilted her head to the side. "I didn't say I don't like it here. It's beautiful." She paused, her tongue darting out to wet her lips. "It's perfect, Mac. Thank you for bringing me here."

"I hope this is just the first of many places I get to take you."

A smile touched her lips. "I hope so too."

The tension was thick in the air around us, but neither of us revisited it as we ordered our food. Opting for something a bit less confrontational, we settled into conversation about hockey. As long as I didn't bring up her past, it was a safe topic to talk about. She wanted to know all about how our trip on the road went and I was equally as curious about how things were while I was gone.

I didn't realize how much I had grown accustomed to her company until that moment. The moment we were done eating and the conversation settled like dust around our feet. There was a comfortableness, a familiarity between us. She took a sip of her wine and her eyes smiled as she watched me.

This was the contentment I had been desperate to find in life. Juliette was simultaneously a breath of fresh air, but also like coming home. Like she was exactly where she belonged—with me. I had missed her while I was away and I hated the thought of leaving again. Things between us could never be like this, but I'd be damned if I wasn't going to hold on to the moment for as long as I could.

Our server arrived back at the table with my card after I paid the bill. I took the folder from her and flipped it open before filling out the tip information and signing my name. Juliette was still watching me with a touch of curiosity dancing in her irises. Tucking the pen inside, I closed the bill folder and slid out of the booth. Juliette moved with me, sliding her hand into mine as I held it out for her again.

"Are you going to tell me where we're going now?"

I shook my head. "You'll see when we get there."

"Okay," she said with reluctance as she finally gave in. Instead of questioning me, she decided she was just going to go with it, which was the most spontaneous thing I'd seen Juliette do since I met her. I led her out of the restaurant and back to my car before helping her inside. I closed the door behind her and adrenaline coursed through my veins as I walked around the front of the car to the driver's side.

I could already feel it.

She was going to be the end of me.

CHAPTER TWENTY-TWO
JULIETTE

My head turned to the side and I looked up at the outside of the building as Mac pulled his car into a parking spot and turned the engine off. He remained silent, his hand still in mine as soft music played in the background. I was a little perplexed as I turned back to look at him with my forehead creased. He brought me to the stadium.

"What are we doing here?"

A smile crossed his lips. "What do you think?"

"You brought me here to skate?"

Mac shrugged with indifference, like he was trying to play it cool. "I could have taken you to a public rink, but I didn't want to. I want it to just be you and me on the ice—no one else."

I stared at him for a moment, a little taken aback by what he had said. It wasn't in a bad way, it just caught me off guard. The things he said or did for me were things no one else had ever done before. I couldn't help but feel a little skeptical, but I could also feel my resolve breaking. Mac Sullivan was tearing down my walls and he didn't even realize it.

Mac got out of the car and walked over to my door to open it before moving to the trunk. I got out and shut the door behind me and walked over to where he was. He handed me my bag that had my skates inside.

"Do you want your stick?" he asked me as he grabbed the butt end of the hockey stick.

I shook my head. "I think I just want to skate, if that's okay."

"Whatever you want to do," he replied with a smile as he released the stick and left both mine and his in the trunk. He leaned forward, grabbing his skates, and shut the trunk. He motioned toward the building with a hint of mischief in his expression. "Shall we?"

"We shall." I grinned back before stepping in front of him. Mac fell into step beside me and we walked over to the players' entrance. Once he punched in a code, the door unlocked and he pulled it open for me. "Are we allowed to be here?"

Mac shrugged. "Probably not, but that makes it even more fun."

"And what happens if we get caught?"

"Are you really worried about getting caught doing something you're not supposed to be doing? He tilted his head to the side. "Are you someone who follows the rules, Juliette?"

"No."

His smile was bright, all straight white teeth. "After you, then."

I walked past Mac and down the hallway that led to the main corridor. Mac reached over for me, his fingers wrapping around mine as he lengthened his stride. My footsteps were rushed and I half jogged to keep up with him as he led me to the locker room. He stopped short by one of the benches, turning to face me as he grabbed my shoulders and spun me around. Laughter filled the air as he gently pushed me backward until he was lowering me down onto the bench.

He stared at me for a moment, hovering above me as he slid his hand underneath my chin. "You're so beautiful, Juliette."

My eyes widened slightly, my lips parting as he brushed his thumb along my bottom lip. Any hesitation, any reservations that I had before were completely gone. I wanted to be here with him and at that moment, I didn't care if anyone ended up catching us.

"I don't want to skate anymore," I told him, my hands reaching for the waistband of his pants. I slid my fingers beneath the elastic. "I have another idea of what we could do here instead."

Mac lifted an eyebrow at me. "Is that so?"

Pulling my lip between my teeth, I nodded. Mac reached for me, abruptly pulling me to my feet. "What kind of ideas did you have, baby?" His mouth dropped down to my neck, licking and sucking on my skin as he made his way up to the shell of my ear. "You want me to fuck you right here?"

Linking my hands behind his neck, I slid my fingers through the ends of his hair that brushed against his nape. "What if I do?"

"Mmm," he murmured, nipping at my earlobe. "I'd love to have this memory every time I come in here and have to sit on this bench." His hands dropped down to mine. "Let's move over to my spot instead. I want to see you there instead of having the memory in Wes's spot."

I laughed softly at the thought. "That would be awkward to think about every time you see him sitting here instead."

"No shit." He laughed with me, leading me across the room to where he sat. "He'd undoubtedly be questioning me on my boner."

"Well, we don't want that," I said, pulling him flush against me. His lips collided with mine momentarily in a bruising kiss before he pulled away. "Strip."

Mac smirked, taking a step away from me. "Whatever you want, Juliette. All you ever have to do is say the word and I will make your dreams come true."

"So, shut up and strip then."

Standing in front of me, Mac's eyes never left mine as he lifted his shirt up and over his head, tossing it to the floor by our feet. My gaze traveled over the planes of his torso, memorizing the dips and curves of his lean muscles as he reached for the waistband of his pants. Confidence was dripping off him as he pushed them down to his ankles and stepped out of them, leaving him in nothing but his boxer briefs.

He was literally handcrafted from God.

"Now what?" he asked as he took a step toward me. "Tell me what you want, baby."

The butterflies in my stomach fluttered as I mirrored him. I slowly began to strip out of my clothing, until I was standing in nothing but my underwear. Mac inhaled sharply as I unclasped my bra and let it fall onto the floor with the rest of our clothing.

"Goddamn," he murmured as he reached for me. His hands found my hips, pulling me flush against his body as he lifted one hand to tilt my head backward. "You're going to be the end of me."

"Good," I breathed, nipping at his lips before they collapsed into mine. His mouth was soft and he tasted like wine as he kissed me sweetly. It started out slow and teasing, but quickly shifted into something else. The kiss had me burning with lust and I needed more. I needed all of him. His movements became urgent and his tongue swiped mine.

Mac's hands were back on my hips. He sat down, pulling me onto his lap. His cock was hard beneath me, pushing against me through the thin layers of our clothing. My legs were wrapped around his lower back and I shifted my weight on top of him, riding his dick as I met friction against my clit.

He broke away from me, his eyes hooded. "Get up,"

he ordered, his voice hoarse and thick with lust. "Lose the panties and face the other way."

I lifted a brow, but didn't question him as I did exactly as he said. His eyes were still on mine, watching me as I bent forward and pushed my underwear down to my ankles. They pooled around my feet and I stepped out of them as Mac lifted his hips and pushed down his boxer briefs. Heat built in the pit of my stomach and I slowly turned around to face the other direction.

As I stopped moving, his hands were on my hips once again, pulling me back toward him. "Sit on my cock, Juliette," he demanded while lowering me down to his lap. I let him guide me, feeling the warmth of his dick pressing against my center. A breath escaped me as I slid down onto him, taking every inch of him in one fluid movement. He filled me with his length, a low moan rumbling in his chest as he wrapped his arms around my torso.

"You're so fucking perfect," he murmured against my shoulder as he kissed my flesh. With one arm linked around my waist, his other hand dropped down between my legs. He pushed my thighs apart and slid his fingers against my flesh until they brushed against my clit.

Lifting myself off him, I stopped with just the tip of his cock inside me before sliding back down his length again. His chest vibrated against my back and he murmured something indistinguishable against my skin. I planted my hands on his knees and began to move up and down, taking his cock in and out. Mac's fingers rolled over my clit, circling over and over as he continued to apply more pressure with every motion.

Our surroundings faded away. My eyes fell shut and I tipped my head back as I continued to ride him. Nothing mattered except for the two of us. Anyone could have walked in on us right then and I wouldn't have even cared. Mac was bringing me closer and closer to the brink of euphoria and I wasn't going to stop until the two of us were falling into that abyss together.

The heat was spreading through my body and the muscles in the pit of my stomach were beginning to tighten. Mac lifted me up with his cock still inside me as he pushed me down onto my hands. I was bent over, my hands now resting on the bench.

With one hand still between my legs, he grabbed my hip with the other and began to shift his weight. He took over, sliding in and out of me as he stroked my insides with his length. I couldn't see straight or form a single coherent thought. This was exactly what I needed from him.

"That's it, baby," he breathed, his fingers moving faster as he pistoned his hips. "Come all over my cock."

Those words sent me over the edge. My knees buckled and I cried out in pure ecstasy as my orgasm tore through my body. Mac was right behind me, fucking me harder until he was spilling his cum deep inside me. He continued to move, his thrusts slower as he slowly circled his fingers over my clit. I was seeing literal stars, my body shaking and quivering beneath his touch. My legs were melting and barely holding me up anymore.

Mac slowed to a stop, both of us panting as he pulled his hand away from my pussy. My body was on fire and my clit was throbbing from the absence of the pressure he was applying only moments before. I lifted my head, a ragged breath slipping out of me.

"Mac, I need to sit down," I told him, half laughing at how ridiculous I sounded. Mac slowly pulled out of me and I almost collapsed directly onto the bench. Just as I was about to, he swept my feet out from underneath me and lifted me into his arms, one around my back and the other under my knees. "What are you doing?"

"Taking you to the showers to get cleaned up."

"You don't have to do that," I told him, another breath escaping me, but this time it wasn't from the way he just fucked me. It was from how attentive he was. How he always seemed to care about the smallest things that usually seemed insignificant.

"I know I don't," he murmured as he pressed his lips to my forehead. "I want to."

He stared back at me with nothing but kindness and affection swirling around in his irises. He wanted to take care of me...

So I let him.

CHAPTER TWENTY-THREE
MAC

After practice, I went home and took Thor for a run before settling into my condo for the evening. Three days had passed since I last saw Juliette, but who was keeping track? Clearly I was. I was still trying to give her some space, even though I really wanted to be a stage five clinger and spend every waking moment with her. The last thing I wanted to do was scare her away, so I pulled back and kept myself in check. Even though we hadn't seen each other, we still talked each day, but the interactions were relatively brief. If I wanted things to go well between us, I had to let Juliette drive. I was just along for the ride, going wherever she wanted to take me.

She had been pretty busy with things at the rink, just as I had been with hockey, so we didn't even see each other in passing. I needed a reason to see her tonight and I knew exactly what would work. Juliette wasn't the biggest fan of cooking. I couldn't really attest to whether or not she was actually a decent cook and just acting like she sucked at it. Based on the amount of takeout she ordered, it was safe to say she at least didn't enjoy it. It was already past dinnertime, so food would get her in my space.

> **MAC**
> Are you home yet?

> **JULIETTE**
> Getting ready to leave work now. What's going on?

> **MAC**
> Did you eat yet?

> **JULIETTE**
> No, not yet.

> **MAC**
> Are you hungry?

> **JULIETTE**
> Lol, what is this, twenty questions?

> **MAC**
> Come over and let me cook for you.

> **JULIETTE**
> Say less, I'll be there.

I smiled to myself, knowing I had her coming to me. Thor looked up at me and grunted as I got up from the couch and successfully managed to disturb him. The rink Juliette worked at was only about a twenty minute drive. I imagined she would stop at her place before heading across the hall to mine. Being neighbors with her was honestly like a blessing and a curse. I loved having her this close, but equally hated it because it was torture being this close and not being able to reach out and touch her. I wanted her in my space.

I texted Juliette back to tell her to drive safely before heading into my kitchen to see what food I even had. Cooking was weirdly something I really enjoyed. It was something I could do for her, so I wanted to. I wanted her to come over and just relax. We both lived fast, busy lives and I wanted some time to slow down. I wanted to enjoy the ride instead of just racing toward whatever our destination was. I wanted to enjoy her.

After rifling through my pantry, fridge, and freezer, I ended up with the ingredients to make an entire meal. I decided on an easy salmon dish with a side of vegetable medley, along with a type of pasta that came from a box with a little packet of seasoning. As much as I did enjoy cooking, sometimes shortcuts like that were needed. I grabbed all the pots and pans out that I needed and got things set up on the stove before I began to start chopping the vegetables.

When she finally ended up knocking on my door, I already had the salmon in the oven, the vegetables were cooking on the stove, as well as the pot with the pasta. Her fist was soft as she knocked on the other side and Thor heard it immediately. He bound through the condo, his nails scratching the wood floors as he skidded to a stop and ended up sliding directly into the wall.

I couldn't help but laugh as I wiped my hands on the hand towel hanging from the stove and made my way over to the door. Thor was back on his feet, his tail wagging as I pulled the door open and smiled at Juliette. Her eyes were wide, head tilting to the side.

"What the hell is going on in here?"

Thor squeezed past me and began to push his body against her leg, demanding her attention. Juliette bent down and pet him as she looked up at me, waiting for an answer.

"Thor heard you knock on the door and wasn't able to stop in time before he ended up colliding with the wall."

Juliette laughed softly as she stood back upright. Her eyes were shining and I resisted the urge to reach out and stroke the side of her face. She was so goddamn beautiful, she would never fully understand the effect she had on me. I think it was safe to say that I was completely obsessed with this woman.

"Come in," I said to her as I pushed the door open farther and stepped out of the way. She walked past me, her shoulder brushing against my chest as she entered my condo. My eyes traveled up and down the length of her body, and I couldn't help but smile when I saw what she had changed into. She was wearing a pair of black sweatpants, along with a hooded sweatshirt. I loved her like this, when she dressed for comfort.

I loved the thought of her being comfortable enough with me to not worry about her looks. Juliette Anderson could be wearing the most hideous outfit and she would still be the most beautiful person on this planet.

"It smells really good," she admitted as she walked into the kitchen. I had kicked the door shut behind me and Thor and I followed after her, both completely smitten. Juliette stopped by the stove and looked around at everything. "I didn't know you were all about cooking like this."

I had a bottle of wine out already, remembering her preference for red. I reached past her and poured us each a glass before handing one to her. "It's something I enjoy doing sometimes."

"Thank God," she laughed into her glass of wine before tipping it back. I watched, mesmerized as her throat moved with her swallow. She looked back at me. "We need one of us to be a good cook, and I can tell you it is most definitely not me."

"Is that so?" I asked, a smirk pulling on my lips as I slowly sipped my drink. "Do you plan on the two of us having dinner like this more often?"

Juliette closed the space between us, her toes reaching mine as she threw one arm up over my shoulder. Her fingers drew circles along the nape of my neck. "Maybe I do."

"I will cook for you every night, my love." My hand reached for her chin and I tipped her head back before dropping my lips to hers. The kiss was slow and torturous, yet sweet and tender. My lips moved away from hers, brushing against them as I spoke. "All you have to do is say the word."

She placed her other hand to my chest and a playful grin danced across her plump lips. "Let's not get too far ahead of ourselves, playboy. I need to see how well you cook before I make a commitment like that."

I grinned back at her. "Fair enough."

Juliette stepped away from me and I turned back to the stove to check on everything. She hung back for a moment, watching me as Thor went and sat down on the floor beside her feet. "Is there anything I can do to help you?"

Shaking my head, I glanced over my shoulder at her. "Nope. I want to do this for you and I want you to relax while I do it."

"You don't have to tell me twice," she said with a chuckle. "My knees aren't happy with me today, so I'm more than glad to sit down."

"Where do you want to eat?" I asked her as I turned the burners off and grabbed my oven mitts. Reaching for the stove, I pulled the door open and grabbed the hot pan from within. I set it on the counter on top of the trivet before looking back at Juliette.

She shrugged and glanced around before looking at the barstools at the kitchen island. "There?" she suggested while pointing at the two seats.

"Perfect," I agreed with a nod, she moved to sit down. Letting the food cool, I grabbed two plates and silverware and set them in front of our seats. The softest of smiles was on her face as she watched me bring each dish over and place the food on our plates.

We were both quiet as we began to eat. Another thing I loved about Juliette was that she didn't give a shit about eating in front of me. Some of the other girls I had "dated"—if you wanted to call it that—in the past had always been weird about eating. They'd pick at their food or order shit that was barely a meal.

Not Juliette. She dug in like she was starving and barely stopped to even breathe. She wasn't here to try and impress me. Juliette Anderson didn't truly care what other people thought of her, and I fucking loved it. She was unapologetically herself and you either loved her or you didn't. Whichever you choose, it didn't bother her at all.

She didn't need to do anything to impress me. I loved her exactly the way she was. There wasn't a single thing I would have changed about her, even with her cynical attitude at times and how goddamn stubborn she could be. She got under my damn skin but that was where I wanted her.

"Okay, you weren't lying," she admitted after swallowing a mouthful of salmon and washing it down with the wine. "You can cook for me any day you want to. I promise I will never object."

Laughter spilled from my lips as I turned in my seat to look at her. "For you, darling, I would quit playing hockey just to be your personal chef and make sure you're actually eating real food for every meal."

Her laugh was like silk against my eardrums. "I would never ask you to give up hockey or anything for me. I can settle for you cooking on the nights you don't have games."

I held out my hand to her and she slid her palm against mine. We both shook on it. "Deal."

"I meant to ask you," she started as she continued to hold my hand. I slowly slid mine until my fingertips were in her palm and I began to trace invisible circles on her flesh. "Could I take Thor to the rink with me tomorrow?"

"Absolutely," I told her with a smile as I glanced at my dog lying on the floor... by Juliette, not me. "I'm pretty sure he might like being with you more than me anyway."

"That's not true," she chuckled as she brushed the tips of her fingers against my palm, mirroring my movements. "He just likes to go along to play with the kids." She paused, her gaze soft as she stared back at me. "Thanks again for skating with the kids the other day. It really meant a lot to them. They're still talking about it."

"It was my pleasure, Juliette," I assured her as I dropped her hand and reached for the opposite one to lace our fingers together. "Anytime you want me to, I'll come do it again."

Her face lit up at the possibility. "Could you imagine

if we could get more of the team to come? I doubt my father would ever agree to it, but it would be amazing for the kids."

I studied her facial features, memorizing them and cataloging every freckle and dimple in my brain. "You haven't asked him?"

She shook her head. "I thought about it, but I don't know if I will."

"If there's anyone who can convince someone to do something, it's most definitely you. You have a way of charming people when you want to."

Juliette laughed. "My father is unfortunately resistant to my ways, but maybe I'll try."

Dropping her hand, I reached beneath her seat and pulled it closer to my own. My eyes were glued to hers as I lifted my hands to cup the sides of her face. "Let me ask some of the guys and see what they say. Maybe if we can get everyone else on board first, your father won't be able to say no."

She stared at me for a moment, her expression unreadable. "You would do that for me?"

"I would do anything for you, Juliette."

Juliette was still in my bed when I left for practice in the morning. I didn't bring it up to the guys until we were all back in the locker room, slipping out of our gear.

Wes, Nico, and Lincoln were all sitting in front of me as I went and stood by them.

"You know how Wes convinced you guys to all do something? I need to pull the same kind of favor."

Lincoln's scowled, Nico cocked his head to the side, and Wes smiled. "What's the favor?" Nico asked.

"Juliette wanted to ask Coach Anderson if we can get the team to go to the rink she works at to skate with the kids. I told her I would ask you guys to see if you would all be on board before she brought it up with him."

"That would be fun as shit," Lincoln said with a smile.

Nico nodded. "I don't know the last time we did something like that."

"I love kids," Wes added.

I clapped my hands together with a smile of satisfaction. "Sweet. If Anderson says no and we can't get the whole team to go work with the kids, maybe we can just get a couple of us to go."

"What kids?"

The air left my lungs in a rush. My eyes widened as I stared at the guys and my body fell rigid. Wes pursed his lips, Lincoln ducked his head, and Nico looked past me at our coach.

"One of the local rinks," Nico explained to him. "We were just talking about going to skate with some of the kids in their youth programs."

"What team is that?" Coach Anderson asked him, although I could feel his eyes on the back of my head.

Nico's lips parted, but nothing came out as he gave me an apologetic look. He didn't know the name and even though he had tried to make it seem like it was his idea originally, that cover was blown.

A sigh escaped me and I turned around to face Coach Anderson. "The Wolverines. They play at Orchid City Ice Rink."

Coach Anderson stared at me, his eyes narrowing slightly. "Is that so? I think I'm familiar with that team." A shadow of suspicion cast itself across his face.

I resisted the urge to swallow roughly. The way he was staring at me had me so fucking uncomfortable. He wasn't a stupid man and quite frankly, he also scared the shit out of me. I knew damn well that he knew the team—and the rink. He knew that his daughter was the one who ran the youth programs.

"I don't see why we couldn't arrange something. Community things always look good for the franchise."

I nodded. "Thank you, sir."

His gaze lingered for a moment longer before he turned around to walk away from the four of us. My body finally sagged and my shoulders dropped as I let out the breath I didn't know I was holding.

"I think you, uh, might be fucked, Sullivan," Lincoln mused out loud from behind me.

I didn't turn around to look at him.

I couldn't disagree with what he said.

CHAPTER TWENTY-FOUR
JULIETTE

"Are you sure that won't be a problem?" I asked my father through the phone as I looked through the peephole on my door again. Mac and I were supposed to be leaving soon to go meet his friends for the figure skating competition.

"Of course not, sweetie," my father said with a gentleness to his tone. "It would be great for the team and I also think it would be a great bonding experience for us. I know I told you that I wanted to repair things between us, but we haven't really spent any time together since then."

"Well, that's just something we need to change then," I concurred with a smile. My father was more of a tough love kind of guy, so expressing his emotions wasn't the easiest for him. I didn't expect there to be an overnight change in our relationship, but already our communication has been better.

Through the peephole on my door, I saw Mac coming out of his condo. I took a step back and grabbed my purse from where it was hanging. "Hey, Dad, I hate to cut this short, but I'm actually getting ready to go out. Can I call you back tomorrow morning and we can talk more about it?"

"Where are you off to this evening?" he asked, sounding curious.

I hadn't told him about Mac being my neighbor, and I wasn't sure if it was time for me to admit that or not. "I'm going to this figure skating competition with some friends."

"That should be fun," he said with simplicity. "Why don't we get breakfast tomorrow at Toni's and we can talk about the team coming to your rink instead of you just calling me?"

"That sounds perfect."

"Good. You have a great night and be safe," he told me. "I love you, honey."

"Love you too, Dad. See you in the morning."

We said our goodbyes and ended the call just as Mac rang my doorbell. I ran my hands down my sweater, smoothing it out before walking over to the door. He was standing just on the other side with his hands tucked in the front pockets of his dark-washed jeans. A smile lit up his face as his eyes met mine.

"Well, hello beautiful."

A deep blush crept across my face, the heat spreading down my neck. "Hey, handsome."

Mac gasped and lifted a hand to his mouth. "Did you just compliment me *again*?"

I swatted at him as I stepped out into the hall and pulled my door shut. "Nope. Nothing to see here."

Mac's hands found my biceps and he spun me around to face him. "There's everything to see here."

His mouth collided with mine, his lips moving against my own in a gentle kiss. I moved mine with his, our mouths melting together. He ran his tongue along the seam of my lips and I parted them, letting him in as he deepened the kiss. The oxygen left my lungs in a rush and I breathed him in instead. He was slowly seeping into the cracks and filling them with his love.

My heart and mind waged a constant war against my feelings for Mac Sullivan. It was inevitable. I would be a liar if I said I wasn't falling for him. Hell, I *was* a liar.

I had already fallen for him.

Mac stared down at me, running the pad of his thumb across my bottom lip. "I suppose we should probably get going, huh?"

I shrugged, a shallow breath escaping me. "It was your idea to go."

"I'm regretting that right now," he murmured as he pressed his thumb against my bottom teeth. "I'd rather take you to my place and have my way with you instead."

"That sounds like a brilliant idea," I agreed as I ran my tongue over the tip of his thumb. "But you already committed to the plans, Mac. We can't cancel on them now."

"You're right," he breathed, his eyes meeting mine as he dropped his mouth to mine and replaced his thumb with his lips as he kissed me softly. "Let's go. The sooner we do this, the sooner I can get you naked underneath me."

I pushed at his chest, laughing as he stared down at me. "Is that all you think about?"

"Among other things," he said with a shrug as he grabbed my hand and laced our fingers together. "But when it comes to you, you can't fault me for that. I think it's safe to say that I'm kind of obsessed with you, baby."

"Don't tell anyone else that," I laughed again as we headed to the elevator. "People might think that you're crazy."

He pulled me closer to him until I was flush against his side with his arm draped over my shoulders. "I don't give a shit about what anyone thinks, except for you."

His words warmed my soul.

Damn him.

Sitting in the stands, Mac was to my left and Harper was to my right. She was sitting next to her boyfriend Nico, and Wes and Charlotte were on the other side of him. The two women were very welcoming and even though they were already friends, neither of them made me feel uncomfortable or like I was an outsider. They welcomed me with open arms. I was grateful. Meeting other women who were already friends as an adult was intimidating as hell.

Group in their boyfriends and the whole dynamic of them all being a friend group, and it had the potential to be super awkward. No one made it feel that way at all. The guys didn't comment on the fact that Mac and I showed up together. On the way to the arena, he told me that Lincoln had bailed. He gave a bullshit excuse of not feeling well, but Mac claimed he thought that Lincoln didn't want to be the seventh wheel.

I couldn't say I blamed him because I would have felt the same exact way, even though Mac and I weren't a couple.

We all stared out at the ice as the announcer introduced us all to the next skaters. It was Charlotte's brother Leo and his partner, Aria. They moved to the center of the rink and got into their respective places before dropping their heads as they waited for the music to begin. The entire building was silent as a soft classical melody began to play through the speakers.

I straightened my spine, sitting up straighter in my seat as I watched the two of them. They both skated in opposite directions, but their movements were mirroring one another. There was something so enchanting and so captivating about the way they moved. They were skating in tandem together, caught in a perfect melody. There wasn't a movement that was off-beat or out of sync.

Growing up, I had watched some of the figure skaters at the rink I played hockey, but I was never really interested in the sport. It required so much focus and technical skating. Plus the thought of jumping in the air and attempting to land on a blade was a bit intimidating.

Watching Leo and Aria was like witnessing something so magical, you could feel it prickling your skin. The goosebumps were covering my arms and the sound of the piano playing slid down my spine as I watched them. I couldn't look away. They were both beautiful with their movements and the chemistry between them was palpable. The dynamic between them. The way they skated in unison.

Their performance told a story of its own. They pushed and pulled around the rink as they skated together. He lifted her above his head, and she was trusting him completely as they went through a series of movements. At one point, he was launching her into the air. My breath caught in my chest as she spun through the air before landing perfectly on the ice.

"Holy shit," I breathed, not talking to anyone in particular. The rest of our group was still silent, everyone watching as the performance continued.

There was an emotional pull of it all, festering deep within my chest. This was something that was going to stick with me for a while. It may have been one of the most beautiful things I had ever watched. The music began to slow down and they slowly skated in circles with different movements until they were meeting one another again in the center.

He grabbed her elbow, spinning her to face him as he skated a few feet backward. Her feet moved with his, skating after him until he stopped, and she smoothly collided into him. He stared down at her for a moment as his arms slid around her back, dipping her backward as they both melted into one another and gracefully moved onto their knees on the ice together. They ended their performance wrapped up in one another.

After a moment of silence, a beat of emotion, everyone in the crowd was on their feet, clapping and cheering for Leo and Aria. It was such a breathtakingly beautiful experience. I looked over at Mac who was studying me with a ghost of a smile on his lips. Tears pricked the corners of my eyes as I clapped, still feeling the intense emotional pull from their performance.

"That was absolutely amazing," I told him softly as I resisted the urge to kiss him in front of everyone.

He nodded and smiled. "It really was, wasn't it?"

"After watching that, I feel like figure skaters don't really get the credit they deserve."

"Girl, if my brother hears you say that, he might try to put a ring on your finger."

Mac half growled as I turned around to look at Charlotte. "The hell he will."

Charlotte rolled her eyes. "Calm down, killer. It's a joke."

Mac mumbled something under his breath as we all sat back down. Leo and Aria were the last skaters of the night, and the judges were finishing up deciding on their results for all of the pairs. The tension was rolling off Mac in waves and I looked over at him, grabbing his hand.

"Hey. She said it was a joke." I dropped my voice lower and moved my hand away from his to avoid drawing attention to us. "I'm not interested in anyone but you."

He stared at me for a second as a slow smile curled his lips. "The feeling's mutual."

The announcer's voice came back through the speaker system in the arena. We all listened intently as they started with third place, working their way toward first place. The other pairs skated out to the center of the ice to get their medals and bouquets of flowers before standing and waiting for the first place winners.

Leo and Aria's names rang throughout the arena. We were all instantly on our feet, clapping for them as they skated together to stand with the other winners. We waited until everything had come to an end and the skaters returned back to the locker rooms. Charlotte insisted that we all come along with her down to where her brother was.

Wes was trying to prove to him that he could get hockey players to show up at a figure skating competition. Charlotte didn't seem to care about that, but instead wanted her brother to see and feel all the support he was getting. We all headed down to the entrance of the building and ended up running into Leo there. He was already out of his skates and had changed into a different outfit.

Everyone took their turn fawning over him and his performance before Charlotte introduced me to him. They could have passed for twins and he was very attractive. His hair was a light brown color, in tousled waves, and his eyes were almost like a golden brown. He took my hand in his and shook it.

"Thank you for coming out," he smiled and nodded. "We really appreciate all of the support."

"It was a beautiful performance. It left such a lasting emotional feeling." I paused and looked past him as I dropped his hand. "Where is your partner, Aria?"

Leo shrugged with indifference. "No idea. I suppose she probably went home."

"They're not together," Charlotte informed me as she appeared back beside her brother. "They just skate together as a pair."

"Really?" I tilted my head to the side, my forehead creasing as I looked back at Leo. "But there was so much chemistry between the two of you."

Leo laughed loudly and shook his head. "Oh, God no. I hate her. We both just ended up without partners and weren't given much of a choice."

"So, you hate her, but you're still able to skate

together like that?"

"She doesn't particularly care for me either." He chuckled and shrugged again. "It's complicated. Like you said, we have chemistry. We skate well together and complement one another. When we're on the ice, the way we really feel about each other doesn't matter."

"Talk about a mindfuck," Charlotte mumbled and shook her head. "Okay, Leo. You ready to go celebrate?"

Mac stepped up beside me. "I think we're actually going to head out for the night."

"I bet you are," Nico chirped as Wes beamed at us.

"It was really nice meeting you and hanging out, Juliette," Harper said as she and Charlotte crowded around me. "We should do a girls' night sometime soon."

"Yes! I live for girls' nights," Charlotte exclaimed as she clapped her hands. I gave both of them my number and hugged the girls before saying bye to Nico, Wes, and Leo.

Mac was waiting patiently with the softest of smiles on his face. "Are you ready to go?"

I nodded, my smile matching his. "Take me home."

"Gladly," he said as he slid his hand into mine, not caring if any of his friends saw, before leading me out to his car. As we reached the passenger's side, he pulled open the door for me, his eyes warm as he watched me climb into his car.

And in that moment, I knew the truth.

I was so goddamn gone for him.

CHAPTER TWENTY-FIVE
MAC

The kids were all congregated on the other side of the boards, impatiently waiting for someone to open the door so they could step out onto the ice. A few of them were banging their sticks against the boards and a few were pounding their fists on the glass. They were all chanting together, yelling for someone to let them out.

I couldn't help but smile and laugh as I shook my head and glanced over at Lincoln.

"Kids, man," he muttered, shaking his head as he snorted.

"Were you like that when you were a kid?" Juliette asked me as she skated over with a bucket of blue practice pucks. They were lighter and bouncier than the pucks we used. These were the ones that were typically used for younger kids to aid in their training.

I shook my head. "I was usually the quieter, well-behaved kid. I stood back while everyone else acted like little assholes and then I ended up being the one who was praised for listening and being good."

"Ah, I should have figured you'd be finding a way to stroke your ego somehow," she mused with amusement dancing in her eyes.

I skated closer to her, my mouth dipping dangerously close to her ear. "I have something for you to stroke."

She inhaled sharply, her head whipping to the side and her gaze colliding with mine as I began to slowly skate backward. Juliette quickly glanced around to see if anyone was looking at us, but no one seemed to be paying any attention. Especially not her father. He was talking with one of the other coaches off the ice with his back toward us.

Juliette looked flustered with her cheeks tinted pink and her chest rising and falling in a frantic manner. I winked at her before spinning to face the other way as I skated over to the door where the kids were. They all stopped yelling, their eyes wide with excitement as they stared up at me. I couldn't help but smile as I looked at them and then back to my teammates that came along with Juliette and the rink's coaching staff.

"Should I let them loose?"

Juliette glanced over at Chase and the way he smiled at her was a thorn in my fucking side. I knew they were just friends, but goddamn him. He couldn't seem to just disappear like I wished he would. Instead, he was always here.

The guys all looked at one another and me, shrugging before looking over to Juliette. All eyes were on her, waiting for her command. She stared over to where I was standing, a smile creeping onto her lips. "Go ahead. Let the wild animals out on the ice."

Lifting my stick in the air, I pressed down on the small knob that was on the top of the boards and undid the latch. The hinges creaked from the metal being rusted. I pushed it open, half pushing the kids out of the way, but they were all shuffling around, running into each other, way too eager to get out on the ice.

I stood off to the side as they all came barreling out. Some of them were skilled skaters and they were zipping around the rink. There were a few that had been skating but were clearly still learning; these kids had the grace of a newborn calf. I couldn't help but laugh as I watched three run directly into one another, each of them toppling onto the other as they all fell down onto the ice.

As I closed the latch, I caught Coach Anderson's gaze from where he was standing along the boards. His expression was unreadable, his lips pressed firmly in a straight line. I was the first to break eye contact and ducked my head as I spun around and skated over to the group. The last thing I was going to do was stand there and be caught in an intense stare-down with him. There's no way that would end well.

The guys were all standing by the bench with the group of kids on one knee in front of them. We had a few different teams that we were going to skate with this evening, but the first was the youngest. The little six-year-olds who still had stars in their eyes when they looked at the ice. It wasn't necessarily something that diminished as kids got older, but once you started to play more competitively, that spark dissipated. Perfectionism would set in and there would be times when hockey was the worst and best part of your life.

I stopped next to Wes and listened to the sound of Juliette's voice as she told the kids what we were going to be doing today. We had a few fun games and drills we planned on doing with the kids, that way it would still be enjoyable and a positive experience, while we could also teach them a few things.

She introduced me and the other eight guys from the team who had come today, before breaking us all up into groups. Lincoln and I went to one corner of the rink, while Wes and Nico were on the other side. We had two players in each corner and then one in the center of the rink for the drill we were going to be working on.

Our first group was five little six-year-olds from the travel and house league, who were all bright-eyed and bushy-tailed. They were ready to go and all lined up on the goal line as Lincoln began to explain what they were supposed to do. As he talked, I demonstrated, and then we let the kids get started.

There was a little girl who was a stronger skater than the others in the group. She was still a little wobbly, her feet randomly slipping out from under her. Determination was carved into her face and her eyebrows were set as she continued to work harder. I couldn't help but smile as I watched her resilience, loving how she refused to give up, even though it wasn't something that was coming easier to her.

"She's my favorite from this age group." Juliette's voice broke through my thoughts as she skated up to me. She slid to a stop as she watched the little girl, her expression filled with pride.

Turning my head to the side, I gave her a look. "You know you're not supposed to pick favorites."

The corners of her mouth twitched. "Well, that's a shame because you were becoming a favorite too."

My eyes widened slightly and I shook my head at her. "I take it back then. Pick favorites, please."

Juliette smiled as she began to skate backward. "I pick you."

Her voice was meant only for me and I couldn't help but smile like a fucking idiot as I turned back to Lincoln and our group. I loved seeing Juliette like this. She was in her element on the ice, working with these kids, but it was even more than that. She was happy.

I loved her happy.

———

The night drew to an end and after spending a greater part of the evening skating with the kids, we were all headed out to the parking lot. Wes and Nico both got into their cars and Lincoln and I headed over to our own, where we were parked beside one another.

"What do you have going on tonight?" he asked me as he pulled open the driver's side door of his car. "I think some of the guys are going out."

"I'm not sure yet," I told him, half lying, half telling the truth. I planned on seeing Juliette, but I wasn't completely sure what I was going to be doing. I didn't get a chance to talk to her to see how much longer she was going to be here. She was left to close up the rink and I couldn't help but hate the thought of her being here alone by herself.

Lincoln nodded, not questioning me on it. "Hit me up if you decide to come out."

"Sounds good," I told him as I glanced around the parking lot while he climbed into his car. I saw Juliette's father across the way, getting into his car. Following suit, I got into my own vehicle and turned on the engine. I sat there, pretending to fiddle with my phone and music as I watched everyone slowly depart from the rink.

The last car to leave was Coach Anderson's. I turned off my engine and got back out, my strides long as I moved across the parking lot to the front door. It was quiet inside, as everyone had already left. I went up to Juliette's office, but it was dark inside and the door was pulled shut. My eyebrows scrunched together and I began to walk around the rink, checking the various locker rooms.

Juliette was in the very last one, checking under the benches for any gear anyone had left behind. Standing in the doorway, I reached up and held on to the trim above the door as I watched her. She didn't notice me at first and moved along the lockers. She bent down, picking up an elbow pad before she stood up and saw me.

A gasp escaped her, her eyes widening slightly before she realized it was just me. "Jesus, you scared the shit out of me. I didn't think anyone else was here."

"You shouldn't leave the doors unlocked, Juliette," I told her as I let go of the trim, letting my arms fall to my sides as I closed the distance between us in the locker room. "You're lucky it was me that came in and not someone else."

"Maybe I was waiting for someone else," she threw back at me, tilting her head to the side as she put her free hand on her hip.

I shook my head as I reached her. "Nice try, baby. I already know I'm your favorite."

Juliette dropped the elbow pad on the bench before she lifted her arms and linked them around the back of my neck, pulling me flush against her body. My legs pressed against hers, urging her backward until her body was pressed against the wall. "You're right. It's only you, Mac."

"Good response," I replied, a smile dancing across my lips before they collided with hers. My hands found her hips and my leg was in between hers. My tongue slid along the seam of her lips and Juliette parted them, giving me access as she tilted her head back. The kiss deepened, her fingers fisting the hair at the nape of my neck as my tongue tangled with hers.

The door to the locker room banged open. Juliette jumped, a gasp escaping her as I lifted my mouth from hers. A ragged breath escaped her and my eyes quickly searched hers.

"Ah, shit, I'm sorry," a gruff voice broke through the silence as I pulled away from Juliette. I slowly turned around, my stomach sinking as I met his gaze. "I was just looking for Jul—iette?" His eyebrows drew together as he looked at the two of us. "Mac?"

Realization dawned on him. Juliette sidestepped me, putting some distance between us. It didn't even matter at this point. We were already caught red-handed.

And I was officially fucked.

CHAPTER TWENTY-SIX
JULIETTE

My eyes widened and I stared at my father as he glared back at Mac for a moment. This was the exact thing he was terrified of happening, and I couldn't help but partially feel the same way. My father tended to be overly protective, even if we didn't have the same relationship we once did. I wasn't sure how he would react to finding out that the guy I was seeing was someone who was a bit off-limits. The fact that he found out this way was most definitely the worst-case scenario.

Mac was frozen in place. I wanted to reach out to him to console him, but I was also frozen. I wasn't sure how to act.

"Hey, Dad," I said slowly, forcing a smile onto my lips, attempting to act like he didn't just walk in on one of the guys who plays on his team pushing me up against the wall with his tongue in my mouth. "What were you looking for me for?"

My father slowly peeled his gaze from Mac and looked to me. "I had something I wanted to talk with you about, but I didn't realize you were otherwise occupied."

Mac stared down at the floor. "So, I think I'm going to head out."

"That's probably for the best," I said, nodding in agreement as I awkwardly shifted my weight on my feet.

"No, you're not going anywhere," my father said at the same time.

Mac looked up at me, his eyes pleading for me to help him out. I couldn't help the immense guilt that flooded me. Us getting caught wouldn't really affect my life. Mac, on the other hand... It was hard to say what would happen to him, and I was the only one who would be able to influence my father into making sure Mac wasn't traded immediately.

"Just go, Mac." I nodded again, attempting to reassure him with my eyes and my expression. I let out a ragged breath with a million other sentences running through my mind, but I knew I couldn't say them. I couldn't tell him that I had this. I couldn't assure him that things would be okay—not verbally, at least. I needed to assess the situation with my father first and see if it was something I was going to need to diffuse.

My father didn't look happy. His eyes followed Mac

as he sulked out of the locker room. A part of me wanted to scold my father for the way he was acting. He wasn't behaving like an adult. He was acting like a child, or almost as if I weren't an adult and he was trying to scare my prom date or something.

The door closed and Mac had disappeared. "That wasn't really necessary."

"Excuse me?"

I held eye contact with my father, refusing to back down. "All of the guys you coach are already terrified of you. You didn't need to try to intimidate him even more."

"I'm sorry, Juliette. I just walked in on one of my players kissing my daughter. Excuse me for being a little shocked, along with pissed." He paused for a second, his jaw tightening. "You of all people should know he isn't what you want. The life he lives isn't what you want, Juliette."

My eyebrows pulled together. "How can you say that when his life is exactly what I had envisioned for myself? He is living the exact life I want."

My father's gaze softened and he let out a sigh as he uncrossed his arms. "I don't want to see you get hurt, Juliette."

"What makes you think he's going to hurt me?" I asked him, my head tilting to the side. "I get it—you don't want anyone to break my heart, but I'm not a little girl that needs to be protected anymore."

My father moved farther into the locker room and

dropped down onto one of the benches. Leaning forward, he propped his elbows against his knees and locked his fingers together. His eyes were on the floor for a moment before he looked back up at me with regret washing over his gaze.

"I owe you an apology for the way I reacted in the past. I wasn't there for you the way I should have been when you got injured. I know I already told you that I regretted it, but I never truly explained how sorry I am for it. I never fully accepted responsibility for the way I treated you." He paused with his lips pursed for a moment. "I should have been there for you as your father, not from a coaching perspective. I'm sorry for not supporting you the way I should have."

His words surprised me. My father wasn't really one to dive into his emotions like this. He had expressed a little bit of this before, but never in depth like this. "It's okay, Dad," I told him as I made my way over to sit on the bench next to him. He dropped his gaze from mine and looked down at his hands as he pressed his thumbs together. "I've moved on from that and let it go. I appreciate your apology, but don't beat yourself up over it."

"It killed me to know that I couldn't protect you from that. It was hard enough with you being in college, living your own life, and then the accident happened... I just—I just wanted to do whatever I could to help you, and there was nothing I could do." His voice cracked and he cleared his throat to cover it up. "When you have children, you will do everything you can to protect them. When something happens that is out of your control, it is very hard to deal with that. But that doesn't excuse my behavior. I should have been more focused on you and what you needed rather than my own feelings."

Reaching out for him, I grabbed his hand and gave him a soft squeeze. He turned his head to the side and looked at me. "Dad, it's okay. There was nothing anyone could have done. I was the only one who could have controlled that outcome, but neither of us can go back in the past to change it now. All we can do is move forward, you know?"

He nodded slowly. "I know. I just don't want to see you get hurt again—emotionally or physically." He paused again, looking around the locker room as he slowly sat up straighter. "This is all so amazing, Juliette. I don't think I've told you how proud I am of you and the life you've made for yourself. Even after not being able to play hockey anymore, you never strayed from that track."

"If I can help other kids get to where I wanted to be, I want to be a part of that."

His eyes met mine again and he nodded. "So, Mac Sullivan…"

"He's a great guy, but I think you already know that."

He let out a sigh, breaking eye contact, and slumped forward again as he hung his head, closing his eyes. "That's the problem. If he was someone I didn't like, it would be a hell of a lot easier for me to get him traded or tell you to stay away from him."

"I have a better idea," I suggested as he looked over at me again. A smile pulled on my lips. "You don't trade him and you don't tell me to stay away from him. You let me make my own decision and just let things be the way they are intended to be."

"Juliette... Mac should know that you don't get involved with your coach's daughter or your teammate's sister. You don't mix business with pleasure."

"Does it really matter?" I asked him, keeping my voice light and soft. "Look, I understand what you are saying and where you are coming from, but for a second, can we just put all of that stuff to the side? You said you wished you had been there to support me in the past when I needed you, so maybe this is your chance to do things differently. You didn't offer your support then, but you can offer it now."

His forehead creased. "You are asking me to support one of my players dating my daughter. Do you realize how that goes against everything that has been instilled in me for a long time?"

"I'm asking you to let me choose who I want to date and not tell me who I can or cannot see." I paused, inhaling deeply before finally speaking the words. "I love him, Dad. I tried to fight it, but it's so hard not to. When I realized he was my new neighbor, I knew he was going to be trouble for my heart, but I didn't realize that it wouldn't be a bad thing. I know what I want. I know what my heart wants. And it's him."

"How long has this been going on?" my father asked, his voice quiet with no accusation in his tone.

"Long enough that I should have come to you about it sooner."

He clenched his jaw and nodded. "That's my fault. If you felt more secure and trusted me, you would have told me about it. I'm sorry, Juliette."

"Hey, it's okay. You don't have to keep apologizing. All I'm asking is for you to hopefully hear what I'm saying."

"I hear you." He let out a sigh with a contemplative look on his face. "You love him."

It felt amazing to have the words off my chest, but I knew there was someone else who needed to hear them even more. I needed to come clean with Mac. I needed to tell him the truth about how I felt.

"I do."

"Okay," he said slowly as he reached over for my hand. "I won't do anything to change or disrupt his career. Sullivan is good and not worth losing because of personal matters. If you feel that strongly about him, you have my support. If he breaks your heart, I can't promise his name won't be smeared after that."

I couldn't help the laughter that escaped me. I shook my head at him with a smile on my lips. "If he breaks my heart, you can do whatever you feel is fitting."

"Deal." My father smiled as he released my hand

and took my other to shake on it. "I do have one favor to ask, though."

As I let go of his hand, the two of us stood up together. "Okay, what's the favor?"

"Don't say anything to Mac yet."

I raised an eyebrow with a curious look on my face. "Why not?"

"Let him sit with this a little bit. I want to see how he works under the pressure."

"So, this is just a test?" I asked him, not feeling the best about his idea. I saw the look on Mac's face when he all but ran from the locker room earlier. If I let him sit with this, who knew what it was going to do to his head.

"I need to have a talk with him," my father said with a shrug. "I can be the one to tell him that his position on the team is safe, but I want to wait until after the game tomorrow night."

"What if he plays like shit?" I asked as we walked out of the locker room together.

My father glanced over at me with a smirk. "Well, then I guess you might not want to date him after that."

I laughed, shaking my head. "You're horrible."

My father wrapped his arm around the tops of my shoulders. "I'm trying to work on that... after I bust your new boyfriend's balls a bit."

I missed this camaraderie with my father. It felt good, like how things used to be between us. We were getting a second chance with our relationship and at the same time, he was going to give Mac a chance to show him that his daughter's heart was safe with him.

I smiled as we walked out into the parking lot together.

Life finally felt like I was exactly where I was supposed to be.

CHAPTER TWENTY-SEVEN
MAC

I stared down at my skates, the defeat hanging heavily over my shoulders. A deep breath escaped me and I leaned forward, grabbing the laces as I began to tighten them before tying them. This was it. This was going to end up being my last game with the Vipers and there was nothing I could do about it. Coach Anderson hadn't said anything to me, but I was sure he was probably looking for a way to get me off the active roster.

He hadn't spoken a single word to me earlier at practice and I was too much of a chicken shit to approach him before the game. If this was going to potentially be my last time playing with the guys, I didn't need to piss him off ahead of time and earn myself a spot on the bench for the entire game. I was going to try to enjoy this last moment with them.

And then after the game I was going to talk to him.

I needed to be upfront and straight with him. He needed to know how I felt about his daughter and how she was someone I was actually serious about. A future with her was appealing to me and something I had thought about frequently.

After leaving the rink last night, I kept my distance from Juliette. I was waiting to hear from her after she had talked with her father, but when I didn't get a message or a call from her, my mind began to question everything. I couldn't help but wonder what was really going on. I thought if things were good, she would have said something. It was driving me insane, yet I couldn't bring myself to be the first one to reach out.

I told myself if I didn't hear from her by the time this game was over, I'd have to be the one to say something.

There were so many things I needed to tell her, but also things I needed to tell Juliette's father. I hadn't told her yet, but he deserved to know that I loved his daughter and I would protect her with my own life. When it came to priorities, Juliette Anderson was at the top. If it came down to it, she would never make me choose her over hockey, but that didn't mean I wouldn't.

"Hey, you've been pretty quiet all day," Lincoln said as he kicked at my shin. "Are you good?"

No, actually, I'm not. Coach Anderson walked in on me and his daughter and now I am going to end up getting traded because of it.

Nodding, I straightened my shoulders and exhaled. "I'm all right. Just ready to get on the ice."

This whole situation had me all fucked up. With how jittery I was, I wasn't sure I was actually ready to get on the ice. I wasn't able to take my pregame nap earlier. I laid there and tossed and turned until it was time for me to get up. The anxiety and anticipation were ruling my life at that point. Shaking my head to myself, I tried to push the unwanted feelings away. The last thing I needed was to get out there and end up fucking up the game too.

Lincoln tilted his head to the side, looking unconvinced. "If there's anything you want to talk about, you know I'm here, right? You know I won't judge you for anything?" He paused for a moment, his voice dropping lower as he stepped closer. "I know I wasn't always the most understanding about you and Juliette, but none of that matters now. I'll always have your back."

"Thanks, man," I told him, nodding. I could feel the weight of my reality hanging heavily in the air. Inhaling deeply, I exhaled and admitted the truth to him. "I'm pretty sure this is going to be my last game with the Vipers."

His eyebrows drew together. "What do you mean?"

"Coach Anderson. He's going to get rid of me."

Lincoln still looked confused, like he wasn't following me. "What happened, Mac?"

A deep sigh left my lips. "He saw Juliette and I. My career here is over."

"Hold the fuck on—did he threaten you or say that he's going to kick you off the team?"

I shook my head. "It just happened last night. I haven't spoken with him about it yet."

Lincoln leveled his gaze with mine. His eyes pierced through my own. "Wait. So, he saw the two of you but didn't say anything to you? You can't possibly know how he's going to react or what he's going to do about it."

I stared back at him, dread filling the pit of my stomach. "Bro, there's no way he'll let me stay. He's been giving me the silent treatment."

"Mac, you've got to get out of your head," Lincoln practically scolded me as we all got ready to go out onto the ice for warm-ups. "Stop letting it bother you. It's going to eat you alive. Did you plan on approaching him about it? Perhaps if you went to him and came clean, it could work in your benefit."

"I was going to after the game," I admitted to him as I fell in line behind him. "I wanted to wait until afterward in case I pissed him off."

"Well, try not to do that," Lincoln told me with a smile. "It's better to ask for forgiveness than it is to ask for permission. I hope you're ready to get on your knees and beg for forgiveness."

I nodded, attempting to smile back at him, even

though the anxious feelings I had refused to waver. "I planned on it."

"Good." He patted me on my shoulder pad. "Everything will work out the way it's intended to."

"You're right," I agreed as we all began to move down the tunnel. Lincoln glanced back at me and winked as the team began to walk faster, heading directly to the ice. As my skates hit the surface, all of the background noise vanished. My problems still lingered, but they would be there after the game.

This was all that mattered right now.

Everything else could wait…

The game went by a lot quicker than I had imagined it would. Once the puck dropped, I was all in. My mind surprisingly didn't wander. The fact that Coach Anderson was on the bench didn't even bother me. It felt like I had reverted back to the mindset I had when I was called up from the minor league team. Suddenly I remembered that I was expendable and had something to prove.

I wouldn't say I played any harder or any differently than I normally did, but I definitely played with a little more determination. I was determined to make Anderson realize it would be a mistake to trade me. He wanted me on the team and it was my job to make sure he remembered that before I talked with him.

We all began to funnel back down the tunnel toward the locker room when I heard someone call out my name. Turning around in line, I looked back toward the benches where the coaches and the equipment managers were getting ready to follow after us. I met Coach Anderson's gaze from where I was standing. He gave nothing away with his expression.

"Come see me after you get cleaned up."

My chest felt like it was going to collapse. My lips were set in a straight line, my expression also giving away nothing. On the outside, I looked like I was completely unaffected. On the inside, I was definitely shitting bricks. I wanted to be the one who approached him, not the other way around. He was going to have the advantage on me now and I just appeared guilty as hell.

I nodded and Anderson turned back to the assistant coach. I headed back to my spot on the bench where my locker was. My movements weren't rushed, but they weren't slow. I wasn't in a hurry to get undressed. Lifting my head after unlacing my skates, my eyes scanned the room, taking it in once more.

My shit was going to be packed up and out of here sooner than I realized.

Everyone around me was laughing, riding the high from our win as they all stripped out of their gear. No one really paid me any mind and I was happy about that. I wanted to take this mental picture of my little found family joking and having a good time. I wanted to store that memory for the rest of my life. Playing on a different team, I would find new friends and make new connections, but nothing would compare to these guys and the friendships we all had.

They really had become my family.

I headed into the shower and got cleaned up before putting on a clean set of clothing. My hair was still damp and I ran my fingers through my tousled curls to untangle them before pushing them out of my face. I caught Lincoln's eye just as he was about to leave the room. He made a move to come over and talk to me instead, but I simply shook my head at him before heading out into the hallway.

Nothing he said was going to make my situation any better.

This was something I had to do by myself.

And after I received the bad news, then I would go home to Juliette and see how the hell we could make this work. Unless her father scared her off from me… then, I wasn't sure what the fuck I would do.

Anderson was sitting in his office and I knocked softly on the door that was ajar. He lifted his gaze from his desk and waved me inside. I slowly entered, leaving the door open intentionally. He wasn't always the most pleasant man, but I didn't think he would say anything bad to me if other people could hear with the door open.

"Close that, please, and take a seat," he instructed as he poured two glasses of bourbon.

Fuck.

Following his instructions, I did what he said and reached forward to take the glass as he held it out to me. He didn't say anything as he studied me and took a sip of the liquor. I wasn't sure how to proceed, so I did the same as him before holding the glass in between both of my hands.

"I gather you know what this is about," he said slowly, assessing me.

I nodded. "I actually wanted to come talk to you, but you beat me to it."

Even though he was still studying me, his expression softened the slightest bit. "Well, we are both grown men here, so let's just cut directly to the chase." There was a pregnant pause before he began again. "I know you've been seeing my daughter for a while now. She told me how the two of you met, how you are neighbors and how your relationship has blossomed."

"I know you don't agree with the two of us being together, but I have no intention of hurting her, sir. Juliette has become extremely important to me, and I really do see a future between us. I understand if you feel uncomfortable about this and don't want me to play for the Vipers anymore. I just wanted you to know that regardless of what happens, your daughter will always be safe with me. I love her and would never hurt her."

A part of me wanted to take back all the words I just spoke. This wasn't going as I had planned. I didn't anticipate having a total word vomit moment. I planned on being cool and calm, approaching this without spilling my guts on his desk for him to analyze.

"Unfortunately, Mac," he started, and my stomach instantly fell to my feet. This was it. Life as I knew it was officially over. "You have no idea what I do or don't agree with. You don't know what I do or don't want."

My eyes widened, my heart beating erratically in my chest. "What?"

"I know exactly how my daughter feels about you. Juliette isn't a little girl anymore and it isn't my place to tell her who she can and can't be with. Whether you hurt her is on you... just know that how I choose to handle you ever hurting her is on me."

My jaw went slack. My lips parted, but no words came out. I was literally at a loss for a response because he had left me so shocked.

"As for you playing for the Vipers," he continued, his voice trailing off before another pregnant pause. "I would be an idiot to have you traded. You are an asset to this team and something we can't afford to lose at this moment." He paused yet again, taking a sip of his bourbon. "Everyone is always replaceable, so this doesn't mean you can start letting up. If anything, I want to see you give more."

I didn't know if I was supposed to question him on everything he said or just accept it. I went with the latter, because I didn't want him to take any of those words back. He was giving me his approval to date his daughter, along with the grace of still being able to play for the Vipers.

"Thank you, sir," I told him, nodding as my heart still continued to go crazy inside my chest. "I will prove myself to you every single game, and I will prove to you that you have nothing to worry about when it comes to me caring for Juliette's heart."

He stared me down for a beat before he nodded again. "Get out of my office. Go find Juliette. I'm fairly certain she's waiting for you."

He didn't have to tell me twice. I was already on my feet, setting my drink down. I thanked him once more before opening the door and heading down the hall. I wasn't going to waste another second without talking to Juliette.

I still couldn't believe things had worked out this way, but I wasn't going to second-guess it.

Like Lincoln had said… everything would work out the way it was intended to.

And I was intending to be the keeper of Juliette Anderson's heart.

CHAPTER TWENTY-EIGHT
JULIETTE

Standing in my kitchen, I glanced over at the clock on the stove as I spooned another scoop of ice cream into my bowl. Mac was going to be home any moment and there wasn't a part of me that doubted he was coming directly to my place instead of his own. Poor Thor, he'd be waiting all night for Mac to take him out.

If I had a key to his place, I would have gone over. Mac didn't say anything to me after last night and I did what my father asked me to do. I let him sit with what happened. It was a little bit fucked up, but it was how my father wanted to handle his player. It wasn't going to hurt Mac, so I didn't argue with it. It was just going to make him sweat the situation a little bit.

I watched the game on TV and Mac played really well. Although it didn't surprise me, he played great under pressure, which was weirdly reassuring for me.

Hockey could very much be a mental game, along with the physical aspect. The last thing I needed was to throw him off. Seeing him play tonight gave me the confidence I needed to know I would never be the one to get in the way of his career.

Carrying my bowl of ice cream, I went and sat down in my kitchen as I looked at the clock again. It was almost as if he knew I was expecting him. A soft knock sounded from the door and I shoveled another spoonful of ice cream into my mouth as I got back up again. A smile was already threatening to slide across my lips, but I fought against it, holding it back as I unlocked the door and pulled it open.

Mac was standing there, looking absolutely delectable with his hair damp from the shower he must've taken after the game and his hands in the front pockets of his joggers. He lifted his head, his gaze colliding with mine. His expression was unreadable and emotion danced in his irises.

"Hey," he spoke softly, almost as if he didn't fully trust his voice.

"Hey," I replied, my voice sounding exactly like his. And I knew it was because I didn't trust mine. I didn't trust myself to speak right now without laying everything out there for him. "Good game tonight."

He half smiled. "Thanks," he nodded. "Can I come in?"

He didn't waste any time. I pushed the door open farther. "Come in."

Mac didn't move, a frown pulling on his lips as we both heard Thor whining from across the hall on the other side of Mac's door. "I need to let him out first."

"It's okay. Do whatever you need to do and bring him with you," I assured him with a small smile. "I'll leave the door unlocked."

Mac watched me for a moment. "Do you want to come take a walk with me instead?"

He was acting strange and it had me feeling a little unsettled. Usually he didn't come off as serious like this. I couldn't help but feel a little anxious, as if I were waiting to get bad news from him.

"Sure, let me grab my sneakers."

Mac nodded and walked across the hall without another word. My stomach was in knots as I reached inside my condo and grabbed the closest pair of shoes I could find. I slipped my feet into them and pulled my door shut behind me as I met him in the center of the hallway. He had grabbed Thor's harness and was still strapping it on him before attaching the leash.

I watched him as he stood upright and motioned toward the elevator. "You lead, I'll follow."

My footsteps were light as I walked over and pressed the button. The car was already at our floor so we stepped inside. Thor brushed up against my leg and I reached down to pet him. The silence between Mac and I was borderline suffocating. I wanted off the damn elevator as soon as possible. I let Thor distract me until we reached the ground floor and the doors were sliding open again.

Mac stepped out first, leading Thor with him, and I followed after them, walking through the building until we were walking out the front door. As we reached the sidewalk, I fell into step beside him. The tension was thick in the air and silence enveloped us. We walked about fifty feet before I reached for his hand and pulled him to a stop.

"Mac, stop."

He slowly turned around to face me, his eyes searching mine. "What's wrong?"

I narrowed my eyes on him. "You tell me. You're acting really strange and I don't particularly like the way it's making me feel."

"We need to talk about last night," he said softly, dropping his eyes to the ground before looking back at me. "I spoke with your father tonight."

Based on the conversation I had with my father, this wasn't adding up and I didn't like it at all. "And what did he tell you?"

"That I can date you and still play for the Vipers."

I stared at him for a beat, feeling my heart beginning to race in my chest. "Is that not something you want?"

He tilted his head to the side. "It's everything I want."

"So, then what is wrong?"

He shifted his weight on his feet. "That's a lie. I want more than that."

My breath caught in my throat. "What?"

Throwing me off guard, he closed the distance between us and reached out to cup the side of my face. "I don't want to date you, Juliette. I want you to be my girlfriend. I want this to be official, not just some fucking fling. Or like we're going on dates to get to know each other. I know what I want, and it's you."

I was still so goddamn confused. "Why the hell were you acting so weird then? Why were you acting like you were going to end things with me instead?"

"Because I fucking love you, Juliette," he said in a rush, his tone half angry. "I'm not the best with intense emotions like this and I was still trying to figure out how I was going to tell you, so there you go. I'm in love with you, Juliette Anderson, and I want you—all of you. Today, tomorrow, every day until you decide you don't want me anymore."

My eyes widened and my lips parted as his words seeped into my bones. "You love me?"

"Yes." He let out a breath, like he was taking a weight off his chest just by admitting that out loud to me. His eyes were soft and gentle as they shifted between both of mine. "If you're going to reject me, can we just do it now?"

There it was. The truth behind why he was acting the way he was. Not only was he having trouble deciding how to tell me he loved me, he was also afraid to tell me. He was afraid to tell me because he was worried I didn't feel the same way.

And I never wanted to assure him more than I did in that moment.

"I'm not going to reject you, Mac." Reaching up, I laid my hand over his and stared up at him. "I'm in love with you, you idiot."

His eyebrows lifted in surprise. "You are?"

"Is it not obvious?"

"I mean, I don't know," he said with a shrug and a chuckle that was laced with a sigh of relief. "I knew you had feelings for me, but I wasn't sure if I was being delusional by thinking you felt the same way I did."

"Well, you're not being delusional, because I do." I laughed softly, reaching for his waist with my other hand. "I love you, Mac Sullivan. Even if you are annoying and get on my damn nerves. Since you've entered my life, I don't really care to experience it without you anymore."

"Good," he said with a smile as his mouth dipped down to mine. "You're going to have a hard time getting rid of me now."

"I wouldn't want it any other way," I said, but my smile fell as I remembered that it was my turn to share a truth with him. It was time that I fully opened up to him and let him in. If I shared my past with him, it would really prove to him that he wasn't delusional. "I'm ready to tell you about why I don't play hockey anymore."

He pulled back, his gaze colliding with mine. "You don't have to do that."

I nodded. "Yes, I do. I want to let you in completely, Mac. Not half, not three quarters. This is how I let you in fully."

"Okay," he said quietly, as he stroked the sides of my face with the pads of his thumbs.

I told him the entire story. I told him about how my future was looking when I played college hockey and about the different options I had to continue to play. It felt freeing, telling him about it all. Even when it shifted to a darker part, to when the accident happened after the party, it still felt good to finally get it all off my chest. It was something about me that I wanted him to know.

I ended the story after telling him about the extensive injuries and the amount of therapy I had to endure. Sorrow filled his eyes and I was thankful it wasn't pity. I didn't feel sorry for myself anymore. It could have been much worse and frankly, I was thankful to have made it out of the accident alive. People have lost more than I did.

"I'm really lucky to even be able to skate anymore," I admitted, my voice soft as I continued to look into his eyes. "It took me awhile to get where I am mentally and it was hard to accept at first, but I'm genuinely happy with my life now."

"Words don't even express how sorry I am for you. I can't imagine going through something traumatic like that and having it change my entire life." He paused for a moment, his gaze dropping to my lips before moving back to my eyes again. "You are literally the strongest person I've ever met, Juliette. You never cease to amaze me."

A blush crept up my neck and spread across my cheeks at his words. "Stop it, Mac. I'm flattered, but equally embarrassed," I laughed.

"You're mine, Juliette," he murmured against my lips as he breathed me in. "Can we just go ahead and make that clear right now?"

"I've never been anyone but yours." I smiled as I lifted up onto my toes and pressed my lips to his.

He kissed me softly and slowly before pulling away. "I want to hear the words from you."

The butterflies in my stomach fluttered to life and an indescribable warmth flooded me. "I love you, Mac."

His answering smile was filled with nothing but utter happiness.

"I love you too."

EPILOGUE
MAC

One year later

As I sat on the beach, I stared out at the water, my hands stroking Juliette's hair as she laid with her head in my lap. The sun was setting in the west and it was casting a soft glow across the ocean. The tips of the waves shimmered beneath the light and I smiled to myself as I looked down at Juliette.

It was hard to believe we had only been together for a year. If I were being honest, it felt like I had known her my entire life. The more time that went on with sharing life with her, it just felt so fucking right. I didn't know how I lived my life without her. I must have been walking around like a shell of a person, because the way she complemented me continued to blow my mind.

Juliette Anderson was quite literally my better half.

She slowly pushed away, sitting up as she turned to look at me. Her hair hung down her back, damp from the salty water. Leaning forward, I brushed a strand away from her face and tucked it behind her ear. My fingers lingered on her skin before lightly trailing down her jaw.

"You're quiet this evening," she mused as her eyes met mine. "Is everything okay?"

We were deep in the hockey season and I had just gotten home this morning from a long stint of away games. It felt like it had been an eternity since I saw Juliette and as soon as I got home, I crawled into bed with her and promised the entire next day would be spent doing whatever it was she wanted to do.

I had convinced her to move in with me about three months ago. Much to my surprise, she didn't even hesitate. She met me in the hallway the day after I asked her with a box of her things and a listing for her condo being available for rent. The growth from when I first met Juliette to how much softer she was now blew me away. She had really softened to a lot of people in life and wasn't as reluctant to let people in like she once was.

She had learned that people could be trusted, that she could lean on other people while still maintaining her independence—which was one thing I never wanted to take away from her. I just wanted Juliette to be herself, while still sharing herself with me.

"No, it's not," I told her with nothing but honesty. There was something that had been bothering me lately and I hadn't said anything to her because I needed to make sure it was the right moment. After experiencing the absence I felt while I was on the road this last time, I knew it was time.

She tilted her head to the side with a touch of concern in her eyes. I didn't miss the rigidity in her body as she swallowed. "Okay. So, what's going on then?"

I let out a breath as I rose to my feet and pulled her with me. Juliette looked extremely confused and there was a part of me that felt guilty for that. The last thing I wanted to do was have her think it was something bad.

"I was doing a lot of thinking while I was away and I don't think I can wait any longer to do this, Juliette," I said softly as I let go of her hands. Juliette narrowed her eyes. "I know we both had our reservations in the beginning. You were afraid to let me in and I didn't really want any commitments. I want you to know that I am committed to you."

I paused, reaching into my pocket as I pulled out the small box inside. While Juliette was still in the water, I snuck it from my bag and tucked it into my pocket for this very moment. Juliette's eyes widened and she lifted her hands to her mouth as I slowly lowered myself onto one knee.

"I want you to know that I am committed to us, Juliette."

She dropped her hands. The look on her face was absolutely priceless. "What the hell are you doing? Get up."

A chuckle rumbled in my chest and I shook my head as I flipped open the lid. "I'll get up when you say yes."

"Oh my god, Mac." She let out a breath, her face turning different shades of pink. It didn't take much for Juliette to become uncomfortable and I couldn't help myself for loving watching her squirm. "Hurry up and ask me so you can get the hell up."

She was absolutely ridiculous, but she was completely mine. There was no one who challenged me like she did. I loved that about her, along with everything else. The way she smelled, the way she sounded, the way she looked at me. Even when she was annoyed with me and had an attitude, I think I loved her more. Juliette was always unapologetically herself and that was something I could never fault her for. I wanted her to be that way, especially with me.

"I love you, Juliette. You are quite possibly everything to me, which I didn't think would ever be possible. I didn't think I would ever find a home in someone else, but that is exactly what you are to me. You are where I feel safe and loved and comfortable. You are my home." I paused, watching her fight the tears as they filled her eyes. "Will you marry me?"

She let out a half sob, half choking sound and

quickly wiped the tears from her face as they fell onto her cheeks. "Yes. Yes, I'll marry you." She bent over, grabbing for me to stand up. "You idiot, get up."

"You're so goddamn charming," I laughed as I rose to my feet. I took Juliette's hand and slid the ring onto her finger. Holding her hand, I brushed my thumb over the ring, loving the way it felt on her.

Juliette lifted her hands and wrapped them around the back of my neck as she pulled my face down to hers. "You love me anyway."

I breathed her in, my lips brushing against hers.

"Until the end of time."

Juliette smiled against my mouth. "Until the end of time," she echoed, before crushing her lips against mine.

EXTENDED EPILOGUE
MAC

Juliette was finishing up at the rink and I didn't have a game tonight, so I was home preparing dinner for her. Thor groaned from where he was lying on the floor by my feet, undoubtedly pissed off that Juliette had left him home today. She was running late this morning and I made her even later after I pulled her into the shower with me. I told her to just leave Thor since she was already behind. He was less than amused about spending the day with me today.

I couldn't help but smile at the fact that my dog preferred Juliette over me. I didn't blame him for it at all. I would have chosen her over me as well.

Closing the book in my lap, I set the pen down on the coffee table and rose to my feet. I set the book down on the dining room table, right on top of the plate I set for Juliette. My mind drifted back to that one time, not long after we had first met, when I ended up with one of her romance novels in my mail. She was so pissed after I wrote in it, but she got over it after I helped her figure out what things she actually liked in real life.

Wes finally came through with the signed copy from Charlotte and I couldn't wait to surprise Juliette with it.

I made my way into the kitchen and started dinner since she would be home within a half an hour. Cooking for her was one of my favorite things to do. Most nights that I didn't have a game, I ended up making dinner, or else we would eat out somewhere. The nights that I didn't play, well, Juliette did whatever she wanted, whether it was takeout or leftovers.

She cooked one time since we had been together and almost burned the house down. After that little mishap, we both agreed it was probably best if she stuck to toast and cereal. To be frank, it was a surprise when she managed to not burn the toast. The poor woman just wasn't designed to cook, and that was perfectly fine with me. It was something I could do for her, and I loved that.

I was finishing setting the table when she finally came walking through the door. We now lived a little farther away from the rink than we did when we lived in the condo. We had since bought a house on the outskirts of Orchid City and lived there together after renting out both of our condos. It was nice for us to have our own space like this, somewhere that we moved into together. Plus, Thor had a backyard to run around in, so it was perfect for all three of us.

"It smells absolutely divine in here," Juliette called from the door as she closed it behind her. I stepped into the hall and glanced at her in the foyer. She was kicking off her shoes as she hung up her purse. Her hair was pulled up in a messy bun on top of her head and her cheeks were still pink from the cold. Her eyes met mine and she smiled brightly. "How was your day?"

"Better now that you're home," I told her, smiling back at her as she walked over to me. She lifted up onto her toes, planting her lips against mine in greeting. "How was yours?"

"Better now that I'm home." She winked as Thor came barreling toward her. He was a little late getting to her. Usually he was sitting by the door waiting, but since he was sleeping, he must not have heard her car pull up. Juliette leaned down to pet him, giving him the attention he demanded from her.

"Leave the dog and come eat," I told her, pushing Thor out of the way with my foot. He gave me a dirty look and Juliette laughed as she pushed past me and headed into the dining room.

She walked over to her seat and looked down at her plate as she sat down. She lifted the book up, inspecting the front before flipping it to look at the back. Her gaze met mine. "Wait, is this Charlotte's new book that doesn't come out until next week?"

"Maybe," I said with a shy smile as I sat down across from her. "Wes may have brought me an extra copy that she had from her publisher."

Juliette opened it up and began to flip through the pages. Her eyes were scanning them and a smile was on her face as she shook her head. "You went through and defiled my book, *again*?"

"I just highlighted a few things I thought you would like."

She looked back at me, closing the book as she propped her left elbow on the table and rested her chin on her hand. The bands on her ring finger glimmered beneath the light. "I like you, husband."

God, I would never get tired of hearing that.

I twirled the ring on my own ring finger, smiling back at her.

"Come here, wife. Dinner can wait until later."

Juliette rose to her feet and rounded the table as I pushed my chair back. She fell into my lap as I grabbed her hips and pulled her toward me. Her hands landed on my shoulders, her face inches from mine. "Are you worried dinner will get cold?"

"Funny you think I care." Reaching up to grab the back of her neck, I pulled her mouth to mine. "I want to eat you first," I murmured against her lips.

"I like that idea," she said before kissing me back. "Dessert before dinner."

Lifting her off my lap, I stripped her naked and pushed the plates out of the way before lying her back on the table. Juliette looked up at me as I settled between her legs. I loved having her like this. There wasn't anything I would trade this for.

I was completely obsessed with her.

My wife.

A LOOK INSIDE THE NEXT BOOK

Keep reading for a look inside Cali's next release, a brand-new standalone about two figure skaters who hate each other but are forced to be partners.

PROLOGUE
ARIA

"This changes nothing between us," I remind him as I lift my blue cashmere sweater up over my head and toss it onto the marble floor. His large hands find my hips and he pulls me flush against his body. "If we do this, it doesn't mean I like you. This doesn't make us friends."

"Likewise," he murmurs, nipping at my bottom lip with his teeth. His leg presses between mine, inching me back until I hit the wall of my foyer. "I never said I liked you, nor did I say I wanted to be your friend."

His lips find the side of my neck as he trails them along my skin. He doesn't kiss me, but I can faintly smell the spearmint on his breath, undoubtedly from the mint he was chewing on after practice. He waited until everyone else had left before approaching me. Heaven forbid Leo Wells gets caught talking to me and being nice.

Leo breaks away from teasing and tasting my skin. I inhale a lungful of oxygen as he stares down at me. His gaze is hooded, his golden eyes darkening as he rakes his gaze over my face. It's like he can't decide what he wants to do with me. When he kissed me at the rink, he caught me off guard, but it was also something that had been building between us for months.

I don't have to like him to want him.

My chest rises and falls in rapid succession. I'm trapped under his gaze, but I don't find myself wanting to hide from him. I want him to see all of me—to *want* all of me. My hands shake ever so slightly as I reach behind my back and unclasp the strap of my bra. Leo's eyes widen, his pupils constrict, and I watch the muscle in his jaw tighten as I drop my bra onto the ground.

"Goddammit, Aria," he groans, closing his eyes as he runs a frustrated hand through his hair. His hair falls just above his eyebrows in light brown tousled waves. "I could stare at you forever."

A smile dances across my lips as I take a step toward him. "You don't like me, Leo."

"I don't have to like you to admit that you're fucking gorgeous." He pauses while moving closer to me, again backing me up until I'm against the wall. He lifts his hands, planting them beside my head as he cages me in. "It's pure torture, having to constantly see you—to watch you—and knowing this is all we'll ever be."

Lifting my own arms, I slide my palms against the nape of his neck. "You watch me?"

"All the damn time," he murmurs, his voice filled with lust. "How could I not? You're everywhere, Aria. Sometimes I wish you would just go away and leave me in peace."

Leo runs his hands down the sides of my torso, his fingers trailing lightly over my flesh. I reach for the bottom hem of his t-shirt and begin to lift it upward. Leo reaches behind his back and pulls the cotton shirt up over his head before he throws it onto the ground. My eyes momentarily drink him in, traveling over the planes of his body as I memorize the curves of the chiseled muscles of his chest and abdomen.

His grip lands on my waist and he lowers his mouth to my ear. His tongue traces the outer shell of my ear, his breath warm against my earlobe. Dropping one hand away from the back of his neck, I reach for him, gripping his cock through his pants. He inhales sharply, his breath hitching as his grip tightens on my hips.

"Aria," he growls my name, his voice low and husky, even though there's a warning in his tone. "I can leave now with your pride still intact, and we can pretend this never happened."

"Or," I say slowly as I reach for the waistband of his pants. My hands find his belt and I unbuckle it before pushing the button through the hole. I begin to pull his zipper down. "You can stay and we can still pretend this never happened."

Leo flattens his palms against my hips and slides his fingers beneath the waistband of my leggings. His touch is soft, his hands warming my skin as he begins to push them down my thighs. He trails his lips down my neck, peppering kisses across my collarbone before he starts to work his way down my body. His hands are sliding my black leggings and my lilac-colored panties down to my ankles. He stops as he reaches my chest and lifts his hands to cup my breasts.

His eyes meet mine with a fire burning deep within his golden brown irises. I watch him as his pink plump lips part, his tongue slips out and he slowly circles it around my nipple. My flesh pebbles under his touch and I fight the urge to arch my back. My gaze stays locked with his and he moves over to my other breast. His movements are deliberately and torturously slow. He never breaks eye contact as his tongue flicks at my skin.

He lowers himself onto his knees, sitting back on his heels as his mouth abandons my chest. Grabbing my ankle, he bends my knee and frees my foot from my underwear and pants. As he sets my foot down, he does the same with the other leg. My feet are both on the marble floor, my back pressed against the light gray wall, and I'm completely naked and exposed under his gaze. Leo sits back, his eyes traveling up and down the length of my body.

"God, you're perfect."

Words fail me as he inches closer. His fingers start at

my ankle, skating across my skin, until he reaches my knee. I watch him, completely mesmerized as he begins to lift my leg up. He spreads my legs, hooking my knee over his shoulder. The heel of my foot rests against the bottom of his shoulder blades. Pinning his forearms against my hips, he splays his fingers along the bottom of my stomach.

He lowers his face, his eyes finding mine as his warm breath tickles the apex of my thighs. "Just one taste," he whispers, his lips brushing against my skin. He makes no other movement as he waits. His eyes bounce between mine and the tension in the air is palpable.

My heart pounds erratically in my chest. I pull my bottom lip between my teeth, biting down as I nod. Approval passes through his gaze and the corners of his mouth twitch before he lowers his mouth down to my flesh. His lips are warm and soft like the finest silk. Sticking out his tongue, he slides it along my pussy, licking me from the bottom up to my clit.

A shiver of pleasure slides up my spine. My head tips back, the crown of my head pressing against the wall as my back simultaneously arches. Leo holds me in place, not letting me move as he begins his assault on my flesh. His movements are intentional. Every lick, every taste, every tease, every touch. Every single thing he does to me is calculated. Leo Wells knows exactly what he's doing to me and he has no plans of stopping.

He flattens his tongue against my clit and begins to

roll it around in circles. The amount of pressure he applies is just enough to cause friction. It is exactly what I'm looking for, exactly what I need for that release I'm so desperate for. Leo keeps one arm pinned against my hip as he drops his other one. His fingertips are soft and featherlight against my skin as they trail between my legs. His mouth pulls away from me for a fraction of a second as he wets his fingers with his tongue.

My body instantly craves his touch. A warmth is building in the pit of my stomach. His lips suction around my clit once more and my knees almost give out from the relief. It's like a reward after having to go a few moments with his face between my legs without him actually touching me. My breath catches in my throat as he presses his fingers against my center.

"You really don't like me, huh?" he murmurs against my flesh, the sarcasm thick in his tone. He looks up at me from where he is on his knees and flicks my clit with his tongue. Slowly, he pushes his fingers inside me, a soft moan falling from my lips as my eyelids flutter.

"Not in the slightest bit." I practically moan the words as he works his tongue against me again. The warmth is spilling into my veins, coursing through my body as the wildfire ignites inside. I don't want him to stop. I can't have him stopping and leaving me hanging. "You're undoubtedly the worst person I've ever met in my life."

"Mmm," he hums against me, his fingers slow and

deliberate as he pushes them deep inside me and pulls them out. He finds a rhythm and begins to pump his fingers in and out of me. "Let me show you how bad I can be."

"I won't stop you."

Mischief dances with the lust in his eyes. A groan rumbles in his chest as his tongue finds my clit once more. Instinctively, my hands find his head and I run my fingers through his hair. The messy tousled waves are soft and silky. He applies more pressure and pumps his fingers harder as my hips buck against his arm that is pinning me to the wall. I grab a fistful of his hair, gripping tightly as my orgasm crashes into my body without any more warning.

It erupts deep inside, quickly consuming me in one swift wave. I cry out, his name falling from my lips as my face screws up and my eyes slam shut. Stars dance in the darkness and my body is on fire, shaking and quivering beneath his touch. Leo's movements become slower as he moves his fingers in and out of me. His mouth doesn't abandon my pussy and he licks and sucks until I'm fully satiated, riding the unbelievable high from him.

Leo pulls his fingers out of me and slips them between his perfect lips, licking my arousal from his skin. My mouth hangs wide open, my chest heaving as I struggle to catch my breath. I can't tear my gaze away from him. The way he just licked me from his fingers. It does something to me that betrays my feelings toward this man.

What we just did goes against everything I feel for him, but I don't even care. I want more of him. I want whatever he wants to give me.

He smirks and his eyes shimmer as he continues to watch me. As he rises to his feet, he wipes his mouth with the back of his hand. He breaks eye contact as he bends down and grabs his t-shirt. Confusion washes over me, my eyebrows pulling together as he takes a step away and puts his shirt on.

"Where are you going?" I ask him, attempting to keep my voice steady, although my body is betraying me with my heart pounding inside my chest. We didn't really talk about our plans for the night, but I'm confused as to why he's ready to leave already.

"I have a flight to catch. I'm going to go spend the weekend with my sister."

Suddenly, I feel extremely exposed under his gaze. There's nothing menacing about the way he looks at me, but his expression is unreadable as he scans my body before landing on my eyes again. "I'm a little confused." I cross my arms over my chest and nod down to his erection in his pants. "What about you?"

"Don't hide yourself from me." Leo reaches for my arms, pulling them away from my chest as he takes a step toward me. "And I'll survive. Consider this a favor from me." He pauses, his lips meeting mine before he pulls away again. I'm left breathless, staring after him as he walks the short distance to the front door and begins to turn the handle.

As he pulls the door open, he pauses at the threshold and glances back at me one last time.

"And now you owe me."

LOOKING FOR MORE HOCKEY?

Check out Cali's college hockey romance series, starting with Cross-Checked Hearts!
Flip the page to take a look inside.

PROLOGUE
ISLA

Two years ago

A low rumble of thunder comes from outside as a steady rain begins to fall from the night sky. I roll over in bed, looking out the window as droplets pelt against the panes of glass. A soft glow from my TV screen illuminates the room and the quiet sound of classical music sounds from the speakers.

It's well after midnight and my brother, August, still isn't back from the going-away party that was being thrown for him and his friends tonight. I was invited, but my parents were smart enough to keep me home. They know how those parties get, with a bunch of newly graduated high school jocks.

A part of me didn't want to go, anyway. I knew that *he* would be there and *she* would be there with him.

Logan Knight.

My brother's best friend.

August and I were only born two years and five months apart. Growing up, I idolized him and put him on a pedestal. Even though we were close in age, he was still my big brother and I looked up to him. The popular kid in school, the star hockey player. And because we were so close in age, his friends took me under their wings, treating me like their little sister too.

Everyone *except* Logan.

In front of everyone, he kept me at arm's length and acted like I was his little sister. When no one was looking, he would sneak into my room and hold me in his arms until the sun rose. He whispered his secrets into my soul and marked my skin with his lips. His light caresses and featherlike kisses were only for me to know about.

I was his dirty little secret.

At least, that's how it felt. Even though we never went any further than kissing, I was still his damn secret.

And now, this time tomorrow, Logan and my brother will be off to a summer long hockey camp before starting college. I've seen both of them almost every single day of my life. I don't know when I would see them again. Maybe Christmas break? Either way... instead of spending his last night with me, he was getting drunk with the hockey team and *her*.

Logan Knight was the second most popular kid in

school. He wasn't the star hockey player, like my brother, but he was August's right-hand man. Even though he was moody and broody, he was the glue that held their team together. August was the sun, while Logan was the moon. He shone brighter than my brother, but only in the darkness.

I continue to stare out the window, listening to the sounds of the summer storm as it rolls in. The windowpanes are streaked with rain and lightning flashes in the distance. Tears prick the corners of my eyes and I blink rapidly against the burning sensation, willing them away. I can't cry, I *won't* cry.

A set of headlights shine from down the road, getting brighter as they move closer to the house. The light doesn't quite reach my windows, but it shifts and lights up the side of the house as the car pulls into our driveway. I can hear the bass from the music playing and a smile forms on my lips, knowing that it's August and that our parents will hear from the neighbors about this in the morning.

He always knows how to make a scene with his arrival and his presence is something that refuses to be ignored. The house already feels empty and lonely, knowing how quiet this summer will be without him and his friends taking over the house.

The music falls silent and I'm left with the sound of the storm outside and the music playing from my TV. The melody shifts into a slower tempo and my heart sinks as I hear a lone car door slamming shut. August comes into the house, but he's quiet as he makes his way to his bedroom and doesn't stop by mine to annoy me.

August quietly closes his bedroom door and I pull my covers closer to my chin. Logan was supposed to be with him, but he must have gone home with *her*. His girlfriend. I can't be mad at him for it. He's with her, not me.

I pull the comforter over my head and bury my face in the pillows as my teenage crush rips my heart to shreds. This is what I get for falling for someone who never felt the same way. All of the veiled glances and stolen kisses never meant a thing to him. I was just a distraction from the demands of Logan's life and nothing more.

My bedroom door opens, but the soft sound is muffled out from the comforter. I sigh, turning my head sideways on my pillow. "Go away, August." As much as I love my brother, I just want to be alone.

The door closes and just when I think that he left, I hear his light footsteps as he pads across my bedroom. The cold air from my bedroom touches the skin on my legs, sending a shiver through my body as the blankets are lifted up. He doesn't pull the comforter away from my head as he climbs under the covers.

"August," I groan, scrunching my face up as the smell of alcohol touches my nose. The mattress dips under his weight. "You smell like shit and I just want to be alone right now."

The smell of *his* cologne overwhelms my senses and my breath catches in my throat when realization muddles my brain. My heart beats erratically in my chest. It's not my brother. It's Logan.

I don't move, my body frozen in place as I hide under the comforter. Logan inches closer to me, his chest warm and solid as he presses it against my back. My skin prickles as his fingers trail along the sliver of my waist that is exposed from my tank top. He slides his soft palm along my flesh and wraps his arm around me.

"I missed you tonight," he breathes into my hair. The smell of whiskey is heavy on his breath. "Why didn't you come to the party at King's house?"

Hayden King. Everyone knows him as King, although he's more of a joker than anything. He's another one of August's best friends, but he isn't quite like Logan. They've been best friends since they were kids, but Logan and August were always attached at the hip.

"Because my parents wouldn't let me go."

"Bullshit," Logan chuckles, lightly tracing circles along my stomach. "Since when does Isla Whitley give a shit about what her parents say? Don't play innocent like you've never snuck out before."

I clench my jaw and swallow hard as I resist the urge to relax against him. My mind and my heart are at war and I'm caught in the middle of it all. "It wasn't my scene tonight."

"Well, all of the guys missed you." He pauses as he rests his forehead against the back of my head. "You know that we're all leaving tomorrow morning for camp."

"Yeah, I know," I grit out, my chest tightening at the painful reminder. His words hit a nerve and I instantly feel guilty for not going. They were all like family and I should have been there to say bye to everyone instead of letting my jealousy get to me. "Was Renee there?"

Logan falls silent for a moment, but his fingers don't stop moving across my stomach. "Yeah, why?"

I shrug against him, mentally kicking myself for even bringing up her name. Jealousy is something that I've struggled so hard with. Logan isn't mine—he never was mine. There's no reason to be feeling the pinch in my heart.

"Tell me why, Isla."

"I don't know," I mumble, shaking my head. "I figured you would have went home with her instead tonight."

Logan pulls his hand away from my stomach and brushes my hair away from my face. "I don't think she would have wanted to be anywhere near me tonight."

"Why's that?" I ask, my eyebrows pinching together as I roll onto my back. Logan shifts beside me, his midnight-colored hair hanging onto his forehead in tousled waves. The light from the TV illuminates through the white comforter and his blue eyes shine as he props his head on his hand and stares down at me.

His full lips curl, flashing his bright white teeth at me. "Because I broke up with her."

My eyes travel across his symmetrical face, memorizing every inch that is already stored in my brain. His sharp eyebrows, his chiseled jawline. I move my gaze over his straight nose—with a small bump on the bridge of it from taking a puck to the face—before settling back on his ocean blue eyes. "Why the hell did you do that?"

As much as I hated the thought of Logan and Renee together, it was all out of envy. I never had anything against Renee. In all honesty, she may have been one of the nicest people I've ever met. She just had something that I wanted, but I could never actually hate her.

Logan shrugs, flattening his palm along the side of my face. "I don't have time for a girlfriend right now. Especially one who is going to be on the other side of the country." He pauses, chewing on his bottom lip as he cups the side of my face. "I need to focus on hockey more than anything."

It feels like a punch to the gut, but I sigh at his brutal honesty. He has the same mindset as my brother—and while it might not be a bad thing, it still hurts. Nothing will ever come before hockey. That is his first love. Everything else just falls in line behind the stick and puck.

"You know that I'm going to miss you, right?"

"Yeah, right." I roll my eyes, swallowing hard over the emotion growing thicker in my throat. His words have the ability to warm my soul, but I know that they're just words. How could he possibly miss me? He won't miss me in the way I wish he would.

"Isla," he whispers, slowly stroking the side of my face as his eyes fall shut. "You just don't get it, do you?"

"What's to get?" I retort, attempting to hide the pain with a facade that's colder than the ice that he skates on. "You're leaving for college, Logan. You have so much ahead of you and you're going to kill it playing college hockey."

His eyes open, his bright blue irises staring directly into my eyes. "Yeah, I know, but that's not even what I'm talking about." He stops for a second, a wave of an unreadable emotion passing through his drunken eyes. "You are a constant in my life. And I hate the fact that I'm going to be leaving you. The fact that I won't see you almost every single day. I won't see you sitting in the stands, cheering me on at every game."

"Logan." I stop, pulling away from him slightly. I've already let my mind and my heart get so invested in a guy that wasn't mine. A guy that simply viewed me as a little sister, regardless of all the times he snuck into my bed or held my hand when no one was looking. "I'll always be a phone call away."

He shakes his head, not accepting that. "That's not the same. I'm going to miss you—this."

"I know what this really is." My voice is clipped and tears prick my eyes, threatening to spill at any given moment. "I'm your dirty little secret. You've always used me as a distraction and honestly, it feels pretty shitty thinking about how you've kept this hidden."

"You think your brother would be okay with this? Your parents? Shit, Isla... you're my best friend's little sister. You have to know that no one else would understand or accept this."

I narrow my eyes at him. "Since when do you give a shit about what anyone else thinks?"

"This is different," he insists, reaching for me again. "August is like my brother. Your parents are like my second parents. All of you are my fucking family."

"So, you think you could just play with my heart all of these years and it wouldn't affect me?" My voice cracks and the tears begin to fall. I don't even bother trying to stop them as they stream down the sides of my face. "That I wouldn't want something more than just this?"

"I never wanted to hurt you, Isla. That's exactly why I knew that we could never get involved." He sighs, the smell of whiskey skating across my face. "I'm no good for you. And I swore to myself that I would never be the one to tarnish your shine."

I face away from him, rolling toward the window. Staring outside, I watch as the rain steadily falls in tandem with the tears that fall from my face. It hurts—every last word that he speaks—but I know that it's the truth and sometimes the truth is a hard pill to swallow.

What was I thinking? That he broke up with Renee and it meant we would be together? No. I've been living too much in my head, in this little fantasy world I created. And it was something that would never be our reality.

"Isla. Don't cry, baby." Logan's voice is soft as he gently grabs my shoulder and rolls me onto my back. "This, between us, it was never just a distraction. I got greedy and wanted a taste of what we could have had if things would have been different."

"That's not even fair," I whisper as he brushes the tears away from my face. "You know, I've had a crush on you for as long as I could remember. And you gave me little bits and pieces of yourself, even if it was just a secret. I took it to heart and read into it more than I should have. I thought you felt the same way about me."

His hand falls still on the side of my face. "You think I don't feel the same way?" His face contorts in pain and his eyes are glazed over as he stares down at me. "The way I feel about you is the reason why I can't let this be anything."

My eyebrows pinch together as my eyes search his. "That makes no sense. If you felt the same way about me, you would want to—"

Logan silences me as his mouth collides with mine. His lips are soft and gentle, moving slowly against mine. The way he feels is ingrained in my brain and my soul. He cups the sides of my face as he moves closer, his chest pressing against mine.

I want to fight against him, to tell him that I'm not

done talking, but he succeeds in chasing the thoughts away. With one touch, one swipe of his tongue along the seam of my lips, I turn into a puddle of mush on the bed. His body is warm against mine and he tastes like whiskey as he invades my mouth. His tongue dances with mine and I instinctively wrap my arms around his shoulders.

I want to stay like this with him forever, but I know it will never last. He confirmed it with everything he said and I know that when I wake up in the morning, he'll be gone. My only option now is to take what I can get from him—this one last time.

Logan kisses me deeply, and there's nothing rushed in the way his lips move against mine. He breathes me in like I'm the oxygen his body needs to survive and I give him every last breath. He's gentle and tender, stroking the sides of my face, like we have all the time in the world together. Like he's savoring the moment and imprinting this memory in his brain for after he leaves.

I move my hands away from his neck, sliding them down his torso. Beneath my palms, I feel the ridges of his muscles from countless hours of working out. I've seen him without a shirt before and his body is something that rivals fitness models'. He's not ripped, but he's fit and it's enough to make my mouth water.

My hands shake and my palms are damp as I slide my fingertips along the waistband of his sweatpants. Logan moans into my mouth, his tongue thrusting against mine before he pulls away. He lifts his head, staring down at me with his lips plump and red from kissing me.

"What are you doing?" Logan murmurs, his hand reaching down to grab mine. "Isla. Stop."

"Why?" I retort, attempting to pull my hand from his. "Isn't this what you really want? This is what Renee did, isn't it?"

"Isla, what the fuck?" His voice is harsh and he wraps his fingers around my hand as he jerks it up to his chest. "Just fucking stop it. This isn't what I want and stop worrying about Renee."

His rejection is a straight blow to the chest and my ego. Embarrassment fills me, heat creeping up my neck as it spreads across my cheeks. I want the mattress to open up and swallow me whole. My heart crawls into my throat and I want to disappear from how desperate and pathetic I just acted.

"You don't want me?"

Logan holds my hand to his chest and shifts his hips. I inhale sharply as I feel his erection press against my leg. "Of course I fucking do, but not like this."

"What if this is what I want?"

A ghost of a smile plays on his lips and the sadness of it touches his eyes. "Trust me, baby, you don't. You might think that you do right now, but I'm not going to take your innocence. Not like this."

"Just go, Logan." My voice is small and the pain is evident in my words. I appreciate his respect and consideration, but that doesn't make it hurt less. "Please."

"And miss out on spending the night with my most favorite person in the world?" His lips curl upward into a true smile as he shakes his head. "Nope. I don't think so."

Logan rolls onto his back, pulling me along with him. I settle along his side, resting my head on his chest as he slides his arm under my neck. He envelops me, his hand on my shoulder as he holds me close. We're both silent, listening to the sounds of the rain falling outside and the classical music that plays from my TV.

"Logan?" I whisper his name, inhaling the scent of his cologne and the whiskey on his breath as he exhales softly. "Promise me that you won't forget about me after you leave."

"I could never forget you, even if I tried."

I tilt my head a little, looking up at him. "That wasn't a promise."

Logan chuckles softly as he plants his warm lips against my forehead, warming my soul.

"I promise."

ABOUT THE AUTHOR

Cali Melle is a USA Today Bestselling Author who writes sports romance that will pull at your heartstrings. You can always expect her stories to come fully equipped with heartthrobs and a happy ending, along with some steamy scenes.

In her free time, Cali can usually be found living in a magical, fantasy world with the newest book or fanfic she's reading or freezing at the ice rink while she watches her kids play hockey.

ALSO BY CALI MELLE

WYNCOTE WOLVES SERIES

Cross Checked Hearts

Deflected Hearts

Playing Offsides

The Faceoff

The Goalie Who Stole Christmas

Splintered Ice

Coast to Coast

Off-Ice Collision

ORCHID CITY SERIES

Meet Me in the Penalty Box

The Tides Between Us

Written In Ice

Dirty Pucking Play

STANDALONES

The Lie of Us

The Christmas Exchange

Printed by Amazon Italia Logistica S.r.l.
Torrazza Piemonte (TO), Italy